CATFISH

Nina Foxx

BROWN GIRLS PUBLISHING

Washington, DC * Houston, Texas

This book is a work of fiction. Names, characters, places and incidents are products of the author's imagination or are used fictitiously. Any resemblance to actual events or locales or persons, living, dead, or somewhere in between, is entirely coincidental

Catfish © 2014 by Nina Foxx
Brown Girls Publishing, LLC
www.browngirlspublishing.com

ISBN:
ISBN-13: 978-0-9915322-2-3
ISBN-10: 0991532228

First Brown Girls Publishing LLC trade printing

Cover and Interior designed by Jessica Tilles/TWA Solutions.com

Manufactured and Printed in the United States of America

3/95399-7725

For my young people:
Drake, Ellison, Sydney, Kai, Jouri, Paris, & Courtney.
Think First.

ACKNOWLEDGMENTS

It's funny how after every book, there are always people to thank, even if you have written fifteen. Every person in my life gives me little things that bring me closer to the finished product, and all of those things are important, no matter how small.

My husband, Barry Jennings, reads everything I write (after rolling his eyes). He has been my person for many years. My family is always right there with me, even when they disagree about how the book should turn out, or what the cover art should look like. Lynda Scott, Brandie Smith, Robert Scott, Sydney Horton and Kai Horton are my cheerleaders. They keep me going back to the well again and again.

I'm also fortunate to have great friends. Marcea Lloyd (no, I will not kill the character just because you don't like them), Cherie Enge (thanks for the legal advice), Reshonda Tate Billingsley, Pamela Walker-Williams and Victoria Christopher Murray-thank you for your encouragement and your support. My sorors of Alpha Kappa Alpha, Sorority

Inc., My Link sisters, Girl Friends, Inc, and fellow Jack and Jill mothers; your never-ending support is priceless.

I have a great team that makes each book much easier in my new Brown Girls Publishing Family, Yolanda Gore and Pageturner.net.

Of course, none of this would be possible without the readers and Bookclubs. Enjoy this one.

Nina

ONE

Dana

My father was not slick. I tried not to twist my mouth as I listened to him attempting to convince me that what he talking about was a good thing. We have a pretty good relationship since he and my mother got divorced, but sometimes he was just transparent as hell.

"Dana, you're gonna love this new church." He looked at me all starry-eyed and he talked in that voice he used on me when he wanted something. He looked and sounded the same way my boy crazy best friend, Damika did every time she met a new hottie.

I groaned. "Church?" Since when had he found religion? Our time together was limited and we didn't usually spend it in church. I wasn't sure he'd even been inside one since before my mother divorced him, and even then, he'd only gone kicking and screaming.

He wanted me to say something. So, I did.

"And what's your new girlfriend's name?"

My dad's mouth dropped open. That probably wasn't what he was looking for. I might have been sixteen, but I wasn't born yesterday. The only reason my father would be talking about new churches and religion was behind a woman. I shook my head. He was going to have to text me from hell.

I couldn't blame him, really. My father was a hot commodity. He's a single, good-looking black man with a good heart. He owned his own home and paid his child support like clockwork. Plus, he had it going on - for an older man. Even though he had a teenaged daughter, he was still attractive and dressed well. He might not be all swole with underwear model abs, but he was a catch. Back in the day, he was really into fitness and now that he was old, it paid off. He didn't have a potbelly like other people's fathers, so I was used to women chasing him. They'd done that before, even when he was married, and it had only gotten worse since.

A lot of kids get messed up when their parent's spilt up, but me, I was okay with it. It was a relief actually, because when they were together, they'd fought all the time. My mother said they loved hard and they fought hard, too. The problem was, I remember the fighting more than anything. If there was love, I never saw it. A few times I'd have to keep myself from throwing up when I heard the noises in their bedroom, but even I knew that sex and love wasn't the same thing. Toward the end they would yell and scream way into the early hours of the morning.

"It's okay. I'll go if you need me to." It almost hurt me to say that. I really didn't feel like going to church, especially one all the way in Brooklyn, but it was easy to see how my words had made him happy. Unlike my mom, he was easy to please. His shoulders relaxed and the nervous look on his face was replaced by a smile.

"It's not what you think. I actually used to go here with my mother when I was a kid," he said.

I folded my arms across my chest and cocked my head to the side. "So, you're saying that it'll just be the two of us?" I knew the answer, but I couldn't resist asking anyway. My father was just too easy sometimes. Clearly, I was the one running game here.

Dad fidgeted a little; similar to the way I did when I was about to tell an un-truth. "No. A friend invited me."

"Um-huh. I knew it. You can't put anything over on me, Dad. I've only been your daughter for sixteen years."

He laughed. "You'll like her. You'll see."

That remained to be seen. Lots of kids had hot moms, but having a hot father was another matter. Women threw themselves at him all the time, all kinds of women. They would hear that "boom-chicka-wawa" when he came in and it was all over. My parents fought about that often, like his swagger was something he could control. My mother would get mad and say it was my father's fault. Now that they were apart, the women threw themselves at him *and* me, like they had to win me over, too. And they were right, they did.

I had to admit that I was going to miss the last one. She'd been a buyer for Macy's, and let me tell you, that had its benefits for me. I owed the hot Baby Phat outfit I had on right now to her. She'd hooked me up with clothes regularly, but of course, the gear stopped coming as soon as they'd broken up.

"Dad, what happened to Susan? I liked her."

"Too high maintenance. Can you go upstairs and put on a dress? If we're going to get there on time, we gotta get going."

I was a little upset that we'd be spending what was left of our weekend with someone that was practically a stranger to me, but it was obvious that my father really wanted me to go. I could overlook my disappointment just this once.

We picked up my father's new girlfriend just a few blocks from the church. I sat in the back so she could ride with my dad, and she was very polite. We'd been through a few girlfriends by now and I'd learned to watch and wait. If they made it past a few weeks, then maybe the two of us could be friends. Otherwise, there was no reason to get attached too early. One mistake, and poof, she could be gone, just like that.

If nothing else, this one was well-dressed, even if she was wearing one of those old lady knit suits. Her hair was pulled back into a tight bun, and her makeup was flawless. She looked a little uptight, but was tall and Top Model thin. Her navy suit fit her like a glove, and she smelled good. *Two points for the new woman.* My dad was into smell. The funny thing was, this one seemed as high-maintenance as Susan had been. Another mom-ism echoed in my head. What was that she'd say? *The things that attract you also make you crazy later?* It was like my father was attracted to the same woman, over and over.

I stared out the window of the car and tried to ignore her chattering as we made our way through the streets of Brooklyn. A glimpse into the rearview mirror told me what I already knew. My father had a grin plastered to his face. He liked this one, but then, they always started out good.

"Dana, I'm so glad you were able to join us. Our church has such a great youth program. You'll be able to meet some nice young people. Young people that are doing things."

I rolled my eyes and kept looking out the window. There was no need for all the noise. Now, did I look like I needed a "program"? She obviously had things twisted. It wasn't like I was some kind of problem child. I went to school regularly and got mostly good grades, and I was generally respectful to my parents, wasn't pregnant and didn't do drugs. I'd said I would go today, but I wasn't trying to enjoy it and I made no promises about going again. And I certainly wasn't trying to hang out with no church kids. I had my own life, in Queens, with all the friends I needed. What could I possible have in common with any of these people? Brooklyn was just too far for anything. I didn't drive, and taking the bus or train all the way across town was just crazy.

We pulled up in front a huge, white brick building that seemed to take up the entire block. Crowds of people walked toward it. I was speechless as my father maneuvered the car into a space and we got out. I don't know why I'd pictured a tiny little cute church, in a storefront or something like that. This building was huge, very old on one end, but it got newer as it went down the block. The corner stone said 1902. There was nothing that old in my neighborhood. Across the street, there was a huge parking lot that took up another city block and that looked like it was filling up, too.

Both Dad and Wanda smiled and greeted people and I tagged behind them. Wanda was the only one that looked comfortable, while my father just looked embarrassed. He was about to be on display like Wanda's new man-candy. All the church ladies were grinning at him while Wanda walked with her head held high and her huge pink bible tucked under her arm, without a care in the world as she showed off her add-water-stir family.

I felt crazy out of place. All of these folks were smiling and laughing and all seemed to know each other. Me, I felt like a vegetarian at a beef convention. The best I could do was put a fake grin on my face. I couldn't believe I'd let my father talk me into this. Not to mention, I'd dug to the bottom of my closet to find the dress I had on. I hated it and it felt like everyone could tell I wasn't comfortable with my outfit. I kept tugging at the bottom to keep it from rising up. To make matters worse, just as we entered the church, I bumped into someone so hard, I almost fell back down the church steps. How embarrassed would I be all sprawled out at the bottom of the steps? What a way to make an entrance. I opened my mouth to swear just as a strong hand caught my arm. It was a good thing, too, because the words I was about to say had no business in a church.

"I'm so sorry. I wasn't looking where I was going."

I found myself looking up into the most handsome light brown eyes I'd seen in a long time. I couldn't say a word. Even if I wasn't between boyfriends I would have been speechless.

"He's the clumsy twin. You have to forgive him. Are you okay?" Another voice said.

My eyes darted back in forth, from one bag of hotness to the other. Oh. My. God. There were two of them. Two caramel-colored hotties, identical, except one had a small mole under his left eye. They wore identical blue suits, but one had on a white shirt and the other didn't. So I wasn't hallucinating.

I managed to smile and I suddenly regretted that I hadn't dug deeper in my closet. "No worries." I brushed imaginary dirt off my dress just as my father called me.

"I gotta go—" I was barely able to speak, but it didn't matter, they were already gone, almost as if they weren't there in the first place. They'd vanished, like a dream. It wasn't until later that I thought to wonder if I'd flashed everybody when I fallen. I could've kicked myself as I reviewed all of the things I could have said that would have sounded so much better than "I gotta go." Somehow, I always managed to find the wrong words.

Wanda introduced my father to every other person we met, grinning all the time and holding his arm showing him around like he was the new "it" bag she'd just bought or something. For the most part, people ignored me, and I only halfway said hello if they spoke.

After what seemed like an eternity, Wanda finally led us to our seats, up in the balcony of the almost completely filled church. I scanned the crowd. There must have been over a thousand people in the building, so there was no way I could even think of spotting the twins. I hadn't even thought to ask their names. I would surely be kicking myself for days about that.

"Okay, I'll see you two later." Wanda had a wide grin on her face like she was proud of herself for getting us to our places or something.

My mouth dropped open a little. I know she didn't bring us here to leave us in the middle of this place.

"You aren't staying?" I asked.

"Of course I am. I have to sit with the choir, remember?" She pointed across the church where the choir was gathering. They were far enough away that I wasn't able to make out any faces, instead, all I saw was a sea of royal blue robes, interrupted occasionally by a flash of gold.

I blushed with embarrassment. She'd probably told me that she sang in the choir while I wasn't listening, on the ride over. I nodded.

"Break a leg." My father still hadn't lost his silly grin.

"Okay. You two come on back to the choir room when it's over. You remember where that is?"

My father nodded quickly. "How could I forget? I spent hours in there when I was a kid."

"I knew you sang with that sexy baritone voice of yours. Sing to me sometime?" she said.

My dad didn't answer, but instead blushed like he'd just been caught doing something he shouldn't. He looked at me quickly, then looked away.

Wanda flashed my dad a smile and then turned and made her way through the crowd.

At first, my dad just stood there. I had to tap him in the arm to remind him to breathe. "Dang, Dad. Do you have to be so obvious?" He might as well have drool dripping down his face. It was amazing that he could be so old and still have a woman get his nose wide open like that.

My dad blushed, but didn't answer me. For a second, I was confused by the church-going, obviously whipped man that was next to me. I could barely recognize my father, but I knew he was in there somewhere.

I daydreamed all through the service. I tried to pay attention but it seemed to go on forever. I was so lost in thought, I almost missed the ending. I perked up when the choir sang, though. They seem to have two or three of them and every one sounded like a professional television choir, complete with a very animated choir director and words projected on the wall like we were in a karaoke spot. Between the choir director dancing and one woman who looked like she was about to twerk any minute, they put on quite a show. A long show.

In all the voices, I couldn't miss Wanda if I tried. She was the one hitting the crazy high note in every song. I didn't know if I was going to like her or not yet, but she certainly had mad skills.

"What'd you think?" my dad asked when she was done.

I shrugged. "Well, I can certainly say I can't do that."

He laughed. "I know what you mean. Time to go, honey." Almost two hours had passed and I'd been lost in my head practically the whole time, except for when the choir sang.

I nodded and followed my dad down to the choir room. "I thought you said this was your first time here. You seem to know where you're going."

"I told you, I went here as a kid. Things haven't changed

much in this building since then. That other building, that's all new."

It was hard to imagine my father as a church boy. He seemed so normal now, but I bet that he got into his share of trouble as a kid. Maybe he'd gone to church so much as a child that he never wanted to go now. He must have been a serious church boy at one point though, because he practically marched us right to the choir room, without hesitation. It was right where my father said it would be.

It was packed with people in various states of undress, and robes were everywhere. The whole church must sing in the choir because there was barely standing room. I stood with my back to the wall while he went to find Wanda. Three hundred different church lady perfume scents attacked my nose all at the same time. Good thing it wasn't too warm. If it were summer, I'd be gagging all over the place. Dad owed me big time for this one.

I stood there, staring into space, when all of a sudden, my eyes focused by themselves. Mr. Fine was no more than a few feet away from me, talking to a group of kids. My breath caught in my throat. It oughta be a crime to look that good. My mother always says God is good, and you know she ain't never lied this time. *God was so good he did it twice.* I took a quick look around for Mr. G.Q's double but he was nowhere to be seen. I hadn't really seen a guy in a suit that looked this good for a long time. Every time my mother tried to get me to go to church lately, I found an excuse not to go, and the guys at school day wore gear that was fresh, but nothing that looked like this. In another situation, I might say that the suits were corny, but these boys looked hot.

I stood taller and sucked in my stomach. Since I wasn't falling down any steps, I felt more confident and prepared this time. I wet my lips and stared in his direction. If you stare, people could feel you staring, and I wanted him to feel me, for sure.

He looked up right on cue. Butterflies did back flips in my stomach. Our eyes locked, and I knew right then it was meant to be. If my life were a cartoon, there would be two characters, running toward each other in slow motion to corny music. There was a reason I'd come today and I'd just found it. I smiled, and he came over.

"I didn't hurt you earlier, did I?" The boy smiled and exposed dimples as deep as the Grand Canyon.

I shook my head. "My lawyer will be contacting you."

"You got jokes." He paused. "That's good. "You tell him to call Jeffrey Barnes."

The name echoed inside my head. *Jeffrey*. "And how will he reach you?" If I could have patted myself on the back for that one, I would have. Like I said, I'd had some time to think, and I was ready.

Jeffrey grinned and told me his number. I took out my cell phone and punched it into my phone and saved it, then gave him mine. "I'm Dana Banks."

"First time here?"

"Of course it's her first time, you ain't never seent her before," some girl said, approaching us. "I know you can read that name tag because you claim to be on the honor roll."

She pointed to the big blue visitor sticker on my shoulder that they'd given us when we came in. It screamed "visitor" big as day.

The grating voiced-girl walked from behind him. She stood just a little too close, hovering over Jeffrey like a security guard. She practically raked her eyes over me as she flipped her long weave over her shoulder. It started at black at her roots and then faded to some blonde-beige combination at the ends. She was pretty, but she wore a ton of makeup, more than my parents would ever allow, and she had bad skin, covered with the remains of pimples. And then, not to mention, how she'd strung her words together, she could barely speak the English language. It took everything I had not to tell her that there was no such word as *seent*.

"I came with my father." I hadn't been in the building three minutes and someone was already tripping. I was surprised to hear the venom in her voice, but I wasn't about to let her see me shook. How could you possibly dislike someone so much and you haven't even met them? It was my turn to rake my eyes over her. Her hair was the best thing she had going for her because from the looks of things, she loved to eat.

"This is my friend, Michelle." Jeffrey blushed.

Michelle practically pushed him out of the way to get closer. "Yes, I'm his *girl*friend. We glad you could visit. Do you think you'll be back?" She spat her words at me.

Jeffrey fidgeted like he was embarrassed. Our eyes met over her shoulder. I hadn't planned on coming back, but it looked like I had a reason to come back now. She was challenging me, and one thing I was not, was afraid. I wouldn't be my father's daughter if I passed up a challenge.

"You know, I think I will." A wide smiled spread across my face. "Your choir is off the chain."

Michelle's eyes opened wide and if I didn't know better, I would say that Jeffrey was trying not to laugh. It was obviously on. And I couldn't wait to make good on my promise.

TWO
Damika

Y ou are smart, you are kind, you are intelligent." I talked
to myself and nodded with each statement, following
my head movements in the mirror, ignoring the pock-marks
that jacked up my skin. I had to give myself my own props
because I didn't have a nanny like that little white kid in *The
Help* movie to remind me every day. And yes, I was all of
those things. Before my father died, he used to tell me how
smart I was all the time and remind me that a girl had to
know what she had going for her so she could use what she
had to her advantage. Well, I knew what my strengths and
weaknesses were. I practiced the Golden Rule almost always,
got straight A's, and could think my way out of any situation.
All of those things were good and I had no doubt they could
take me far.

What I was not though, was pretty. I'm not even good-
looking, not like my girl, Dana. Dana was thin, with long
hair, great skin and great clothes. I was short and round

with hair like Brillo. I was, as Dana would say, hair-dresser challenged."

My mother wasn't really a shopper so my clothing was basic. I was cool with all that, though. Overall, I liked me. I knew exactly where I fit all the time and definitely wasn't trying to impress anyone. I wasn't ever going to fit in with the cool, popular kids, but I was good with that, too.

No sooner had I jumped back into bed, than my mother knocked on my bedroom door and peeked her head in. "You still in bed, pumpkin?"

I pulled my covers up to my neck. She knew I was up. I'd been listening to her move around for at least an hour now, but I hadn't budged at all. "Yup."

"I guess this means you aren't going to church this morning?"

"Umh umm." But she knew that, too. I didn't mind going actually, but my mother would stay all day, and I mean *all* day. It wasn't even seven AM, but once she left, I knew she'd be gone at least twelve hours.

"You have a lot of homework?"

We had this same conversation every week, but she only made me go like once a month. I figured that between Sunday school, worship service and meetings, her church day was four times as long as everyone else's. I was good.

"I have a report to finish."

She paused, then answered what I knew she would. "Okay then. You call me if you have to leave the house before I get back. Don't leave though, unless you absolutely have to, and don't let anyone in. I'll pray for you."

I nodded in agreement like this was a new thing. My mother did more praying for me than she did talking to me, and she treated me like I was a little kid most of the time. I rarely got to go anywhere without her, and I certainly couldn't have company without jumping through all kinds of hoops, especially company when she didn't know their parents.

I waited for her to shut the door and then sat up in my bed, listening. I wasn't going to get out of bed until I was sure that she had driven off this street. Like I said, I was intelligent, and I'd certainly learned what I needed to do to survive. If I moved too fast, they might be tempted to wait for me or something, and we didn't want that. I had plans today. My friends were waiting.

Ten years ago, I would have been a lonely teenager, for sure. Thanks to modern technology and a state of the art Mac Book Pro that my Mom bought with the insurance money from my Dad's policy, I had lots of friends. I was on Facebook and Twitter and I had a Tumblr blog. On my phone, I used SnapChat and Kik. I'd even tried Second Life, but I didn't like that too much.

It only took a few minutes for the house to be deadly silent. The loudest sound in the house was the ticking of my pink watch. Mama didn't mess around when it came to getting her church on. I rolled out of bed, stretched, then took a few minutes to try and make my short 'fro the same on all sides. Dana was always trying to get me to get a perm or a weave, but that was too much like work. I looked like what I was supposed to look like, and I knew my mother wasn't going to agree to keep putting out money to do all that no way. She said that school was not a fashion show, and she was right. Besides, I had a friend or two that really didn't care what my hair looked like, but I was just trying to shove it into place in case I ended up video chatting on Ovoo. Sunday was the day I usually met Rosheon online.

Rosheon was my secret. No one knew about him, even Dana. I just started video chatting with him about a month ago. Before that, we'd only typed back and forth or chatted on Facebook. That's how I met him. He was a friend of a friend of a friend and was always commenting on stuff I said, then one day, he friended me. Dana almost lost her mind when I told her that I friended someone I didn't know, so I never told her any of the details. She claims she never friended anyone she didn't know, but I knew that Rosheon was cool. I was so surprised when I met him, though, because he looked nothing like he sounded. Rosheon was fine. I almost couldn't' believe that hottie like him was even interested in me, but he was. He said he was crazy about me, inside and out, and

I believed him. He wasn't stupid like those knuckleheads at school.

In real life, I might have been "just basic", but online, I could be anyone I wanted to be. When I walked down the hall at Hillcrest High School, I was invisible, but in Cyberspace, Damika Woods was a star.

THREE

Dana

My dad dropped me off as usual, and I left my bag at the door and was on the way to my room when my mother stopped me.

"Hey, hey. Don't you have any love for your mother?"

Like many Sunday's since the divorce, my mom hadn't gotten dressed. She still had on her pink pajamas and she had a wine glass in her hand. She always had a glass in her hand now if she was at home. For someone who was supposed to be churchgoing, my mother, believed in the grapes, especially on the weekends. Especially since the divorce. She counted them as vegetables in her well-balanced diet.

"Hi, Mom." I slowed down and tried not to look too happy. She was going to have a lot of questions. My father had to get special permission to bring me back late, and she was going to want to question me about the reason for sure. They both did that, tried to get information about the other one through me, and I hated it, although my mother did it more. I couldn't understand how two grown people that had lived together for twenty years couldn't just come right out and ask each other what they wanted to know, especially since she was the one who'd asked Daddy to leave.

She wasn't always this way. My mother used to be real happy. The thing was, I couldn't tell whether her unhappiness was due to the divorce or because after daddy left, she had to go back to work. It used to be that my mother was the only one on the block who didn't have to work, and as far as I could tell, she liked it that way. We used to spend so much more time shopping and stuff like that, but now I was lucky to get to the mall with her once a month, if then. Now, what shopping she did do, she mostly did online. She was also tired all the time, too tired to be bothered with running me back and forth to the mall or anything.

Don't get me wrong, my mother was a smart woman. Her and my dad met at the office. She was a paralegal and worked in his office. After they got married, she stayed home and took care of me. Until Mom and Dad started fighting, I remember her as being happy all the time. When she asked daddy to leave, she did the math, and she had to go out and get a job. Some days, I couldn't tell what made her more unhappy; being man-less, or having to go to work every day with people she didn't really like and then coming home to gripe about who did what to whom while she was there.

My mother wrapped her arms around me and I held my breath. I didn't want to smell her yeasty, unwashed smell as it mixed with the alcohol on her breath. I would be glad when she snapped out of the funk she'd been in for the past few months. I didn't need to be no psychologist to see she was depressed. From the way she acted, you'd think that my father had divorced her and not the other way around. As far as I was concerned, her unhappiness was her own doing.

"So, your father said you two went to church together." When she started out with "so", she was usually prepared to wait for an answer, no matter how long it took me. A question hung in her voice and I knew she wasn't going to let me ignore it.

I nodded.

"What's *she* like?"

"Who?" I really hated being in the middle.

"Don't play games, Dana."

"I don't know what you mean, Mom. We went to the church Dad went to when he was growing up." My eyes were wide as I tried not to blink. The last thing I wanted was for my parents to get into it over going to church. I had no idea why I was covering for my father, and I wasn't really sure if Mom cared or not. In my opinion, if you kick someone to the curb, you need to just keep on stepping, but of course, no one asked me.

She raised her eyebrows at me. She was thinking over what I'd just told her.

I didn't want her to think too long. "I've got to double check my work for school tomorrow." It was best just to cut her off. She wouldn't want to talk about it in the morning. Or at least I hoped she wouldn't.

It took a minute, but she finally stepped out of my way and I let out the breath that I'd been holding.

"Take your bag upstairs with you. There are no maids here."

And there she was. The mom I'd become accustomed to, the one who never heard what I said or cared what I thought. I rolled my eyes, grabbed the bag and headed upstairs to call Damika. I had to let her know that she would be going to church next weekend.

Damika was waiting for me to call. She listened silently at first as I described the twins.

"You couldn't find no good looking ones in Queens? Dang. Neither one of us drives and you know I hate the subway. Why do we have to go all the way to Brooklyn?" she whined.

"Girl, it's just across town. You act like we Brooklyn is five hours away or something."

Times like this I wished we lived down south or something. All of my cousins had driver's licenses, if not cars, by the time they were sixteen. Some of them even drove to school every day. Thanks to driver's Ed, I could drive, but there was no way my folks could afford to even think about getting me a car. The insurance alone would kill us.

"Think about what I'm saying. Twins. One for me and one for you."

"You don't even know that the other one will feel me like that."

I hated when Damika talked like this. Sometimes, she just didn't know how cute she really was. She was forever putting herself down.

"Just stop," I said. "What's not to like?"

"All right. But I better not get the boring one this time."

"Twins, girl. *Twins*. And you can tell your parents that my father will drive us."

Damika's mother was the strictest parent I knew. She would put a tracking device on her if she thought we'd be riding the train all the way to Brooklyn, especially to meet a boy. It just wasn't going to happen.

I hung up the phone just as voices drifted up from downstairs. My mother was arguing with someone, no doubt with that trifling man she was seeing. Unlike my father, she'd been seeing the same guy since the divorce, but I don't even know why she was wasting her time with him. He didn't treat her nice and they argued all the time. It didn't even seem like they really got along. I made my way downstairs to see what all the commotion was about.

They looked up as I tried to peek my way into the kitchen, then turned back to the evil looks they were giving each other. My mother was sitting at the table and he was leaning back on the sink with both of his arms crossed in front of him. I really didn't want to interrupt them, but I needed to lay the seed now for going to church with my father next week.

"Mom," I said. "Can I talk to you for a minute?"

They stopped talking, but neither of them budged. "I was hoping for some privacy." I kept my eyes trained on the boyfriend, Dennis.

"You can say anything you need to in front of Dennis. He's practically family."

He's not, I thought. I wanted to wipe that stupid gloating look off his face.

"Well, I want to ask you if Dad can have next Sunday, too."

A look of shock came over my mother's face. I looked away. She looked like I'd hit her or something instead of just asked to spend time with my own father.

"I had plans for us."

I doubted that.

"You should let her go. It's good for a teenager to bond with her father. And didn't you say he took her to church?"

It was my turn to be shocked. Dennis was taking up for me and I know he didn't even like me. He just tolerated me enough to make my mother happy, and he barely did that.

He was probably trying to get rid of me again, but as long as I got to go, all was good. I didn't care what his motives were. I tried to smile.

"Yes, we're going to church *again*. I liked it."

My mother took a sip from her glass, and I held my breath while I waited for her to make up her mind. *Please, please, please.*

"You liked church?"

I nodded.

"Just make sure you're back early. Right after."

It's a good thing she didn't pick now to go into some long sermon about my father. She already thought he didn't respect the rules enough, but I really didn't care. Their stuff was theirs and I didn't want to be in it. All I really cared about was how it would impact me. I kissed my mother on the cheek.

"Thank you. I will."

"And tell your father to call me so we can discuss it. I can't have him keeping you out late every week."

I didn't understand why she couldn't just call him herself, but I didn't say that. It's not like they hadn't been married to each other since dirt. I made eye contact with Dennis before I left. He nodded at me, but didn't smile, and a shiver ran down my spine.

FOUR
Damika

Dana and I have been best friends since third grade, but she doesn't always get me. I listened to her when she was rambling on the phone about the hotties she'd met with her Dad, and although I didn't really want to go all the way to Brooklyn, I agreed. The two of us are real tight and I know she'd do the same for me. It'd been that way between us since the day we met.

It was my first day in a new school, and some big kids were hassling me. That day, they were teasing me about my lunchbox, the one my mother insisted I take, even though I just wanted to take my lunch in a brown paper bag. Dana had walked right up to those big girls and told them where they could go. I was so scared for both of us then, but Dana showed me that sometimes if you act like you pack a big punch, people will believe it.

It wouldn't hurt to go along with her game for a minute, even figure out a way to let my folks let me go, because I know my turn was coming fast - a time when she was going to have to stand up or lie for me. That's just how we roll.

As soon as we hung up, my phoned buzzed. A huge smile crossed my face. It was my boo.

"Rosheon. I wasn't expecting to hear from you," I sang after answering the phone. I'm usually the practical one out of me and Dana, but since I met Ro, I'd been sprung. Just talking to him made me feel all special. My heart was all racing and stuff. I waited for him online practically all day, but he'd never showed. I wasn't mad though. He wasn't a prisoner in his house like I was.

"I know, that's why I'm here."

His words didn't register immediately. "Here?" I said. "Here where?"

"In front of your house. Come out and see me."

I glanced at the clock and panicked. It was almost seven on a Sunday. "I'm not sure that's such a good idea." Right now, my mother was still at church, but I didn't know how long that would last. She was on the board of trustees and sometimes she stayed late for meetings on Sunday evenings. Today was one of those times, but the thing was, I had no idea how long the meetings would be. It could be as short as a half hour, or as long as a few.

My mind whirred. No one had met Rosheon yet. Not my parents, not even Dana. They didn't even know about him, so it wouldn't be good for them to drive up and see me sitting outside with him in his car. My mother would trip. Not only was he a stranger and I was supposed to be inside studying, doing homework and making sure that dinner was ready when she came in, but Rosheon was a little older than most boys my age. Okay, a lot older. Eight years, to be exact. I knew that age had nothing to do with how I felt about Rosheon, but I definitely couldn't see my mother understanding.

Rosheon seemed to sense my uneasiness. "Look, I ain't trying to get you in trouble. I won't stay long, I just have something I want to give you, that's all."

A grin spread across my face. "Just for a minute, then."

Rosheon used to send me little gifts on Facebook, but ever since we'd met in person a few weeks ago, he'd graduated to real gifts. They usually weren't a big deal or anything, but they meant a lot to me. A flower, a nice book. He'd leave them on the doorstep, or in the mailbox and I'd break my neck to find them before my parents did. It freaked me out at first, because I hadn't really told him where I lived.

"You gave me enough information to find you." That's what he told me when I'd asked him. I'd wondered about it for hours until I realized that one of the pictures I'd sent him had been standing in front of my house. He didn't say, but he probably found me because of my iPhone.

Rosheon was very thoughtful in the few weeks I'd known him, even though he looked nothing like the picture of himself that he'd posted on *Hot or Not*. In fact, he was much older and heavier than that picture. I fell for his Catfish Okee doke. There were no washboard abs, no eyes damn near the color of an emerald, but I got over that fast. He was just so caring. His picture might not look like him in person, but underneath, he was the same person I'd met online. None of the boys I messed with before ever gave me anything and it made me feel special. Not that there had been a lot of boys that I'd messed with. I wasn't exactly in high demand, not like Dana. But that was what made him different. Rosheon wasn't a boy, he was a man.

I hopped off my bed and quickly checked my hair and teeth in the mirror, then said a short prayer that my mother would stay out just awhile longer. It wasn't unusual for her meetings at church to run late.

My mother wasn't strict. There's no word in the English language for what she was. She's beyond strict, almost a prison warden. In fact, that is what Dana and I called her sometimes. She just didn't think I needed to be talking to any boys at all. None. All she cared about was me getting into college and getting good grades in school. If she came home and saw me talking to Rosheon, I might as well kiss my narrow butt goodbye. She'd probably send me to military school or ground me until I was thirty.

I ran downstairs, made a quick dash from my front steps to the car. I hopped in beside Rosheon. His car was special, to say the least. Technically, it was a beater, an old car that he'd fixed up, but it was hot. He carpeted the inside in retro shag, even the dashboard, and it smelled good. He always had a crown air freshener going. Rosheon smelled and looked good, too. He had on a nice, powder blue shirt that looked like he'd just ironed it, even though I knew he'd probably put it on for church that morning. Sharp was his trademark. He leaned over to kiss me hello and I looked around quickly. I let him give me a fast peck on the lips. This was no place for me to be caught with his tongue down my throat. My nosey neighbors were probably watching and would report to my mother, anyway, especially that Glodean Miller that lived right across the street. She didn't have a job or anything, all she seemed to do was sit in her house, up in the window and spy on me and the other kids that lived on my block. That woman was Neighborhood Watch all by herself.

I was nervous, but I still broke into a grin when his cheek rubbed against mine. I loved the way Rosheon's face felt late in the evening. All stubbly and rough. I really only had one boyfriend before and we'd barely kissed, but it wasn't the same. Not one of them had any serious facial hair.

"Hey, baby," I said. "What are you doing here?" I was a little scared, but still excited to see him.

Rosheon sniffed my hair. He said he loved the way I smelled and when he did that my stomach turned flips.

"I had to see you. I needed a fix."

I hit him in the arm. "Could you not compare me to a drug, please?" I teased him, but inside I loved that he thought of me as something he couldn't do without.

"You might as well be. Once I got a hit I couldn't put you down."

Now, I might be young, but even I knew that line was corny as hell. Still, my face felt warm. "Stop it. My folks'll be home soon."

"I know. I won't keep you long. I just wanted you to have something." He reached behind the seat and pulled up a small shopping bag with tissue paper coming out of the top.

My mouth dropped open. This didn't look like any small token. Rosheon had bought me stationary before and a nice pen, but nothing that had come in a jewelry store bag.

"What's this?" My voice trembled.

"A little something I saw and thought of you. No big deal." He grinned. "I thought you said you were in a hurry. You gonna open it or what?"

Or what. My brain screamed at me that I should refuse the gift. I knew, without a doubt, that my mother would disapprove of me taking gifts from Rosheon. He pushed the bag in my direction and I took it. My hand trembled a little, but I wasn't sure if that was because I was excited, or scared. There would be no harm in opening it, even if I gave it back after. I had to at least *see* what I was going to be turning down.

Rosheon watched as I pulled the tissue from the bag and a small box fell into my lap. I don't know what I was expecting, but I gasped when I flipped opened the top. Rosheon watched as I stared at the gold and diamond pendant in the box. It was small shoe hung on a delicate chain.

"Like it? I wasn't sure you would."

His words snapped me back to my senses. "It's beautiful, but you shouldn't have done this. I can't keep it." My mind spun. It was real cute, just like the one I'd seen in the gold ad in *Lucky* Magazine, me and Dana's shopping bible. We read it every month and wished for all the stuff we never had money to get.

"You can. It's no big deal. It wasn't real expensive or anything. And someone as beautiful as you are deserves beautiful things."

I blushed. "You think I'm beautiful?"

"He put his hand on the nape of my neck and drew me to him, touching his lips to my face near my ear. "I know you don't believe it, but you have a beauty unlike other girls. You just don't realize it yet."

My breath caught in my throat and I swallowed hard. My mother was going to trip. It made me feel special when Rosheon talked like that, but there was no way I would be able to explain this. She knew exactly how much money I had because she gave it to me, and this was obviously outside my budget. I kept going back and forth with myself, but deep down, I wanted to keep it. With this around my neck I would be hotter than Paris Hilton, for sure.

Rosheon took it from the box and I let him put it around my neck. It fell just right, right on my collarbone. This necklace belonged on me; it was perfect. I *could* always hide it under my shirt. I didn't have time to think about because my phone rang just then and when I glanced at the Caller id, I panicked. It was my mother. If she was calling me, it meant her meeting was over, or close to it.

My face stung. "I gotta go." I hopped out of the car and a chill ran through me. Before I could decide whether to answer or not, the phone stopped ringing. I was dead. She was going to kill me.

"Have you thought about what we talked about before?" Rosheon's husky voice was normally music to my ears, but all I could think about was the look on my mother's face if she saw me out here talking to a man in a car that she didn't know.

I immediately felt tense. I knew exactly what he meant. He wanted me to have sex with him. "Not really, Rosheon. But I'm pretty sure that I'm not ready. I told you, I think I want to wait." My face felt hot. I certainly couldn't talk about it now. My mother could come around that corner any minute, and if she did, I just might pee my pants.

He sat back in his seat and sighed. "If that's what you want to do, I can respect that. I knew you were a little young when I got involved." He smiled then. "But I think you'll be worth the wait."

All men gave you that line, everyone knows that, and I was sure that Rosheon could probably find an older girl to do what he wanted. I liked him, but that was a line I was just not ready to cross. I returned his smile, and my phone rang again. This time, I walked away from the car and flipped my phone open. He didn't stop me. I was glad he wasn't tripping about my decision. Right now, I had much bigger things to worry about.

"Yes, Mom?"

Rosheon rolled down the passenger window and I tried to walk away and talk to my mother at the same time. I waved at Rosheon that he had to go, not looking back for fear that mother would catch me. I wiped the sweat from my palms on my jeans. I was certain that we would continue this discussion later.

As soon as I closed my door behind me, I felt a little better. What had I been thinking? I couldn't quite think straight as far as Rosheon was concerned. No sooner than I'd snapped my phone shut, it buzzed again. Rosheon was texting me. *Check the bag again.*

I'd obviously missed something. I glanced at the clock. My mother was on her way and it took usually no more than ten minutes for her to get home from the church. I had to at least have the table set by the time she arrived, but I put my hand down inside the little bag anyway. I hit something hard, grabbed it and pulled it out.

I gasped. It was a phone. Why would he give me a phone? I already had one. My mother had given me one for Christmas. I examined the new phone. It sure was cute. It was a new iPhone, old, but much newer than the one I'd had. I'd asked my mother for one before but she told me it wasn't in the budget because it wasn't upgrade time on our cell phone plan. She limited my phone as it was; I had limited data and texts, and the thing shut down completely at nine PM. If I pissed her off, she'd take it from me in a minute, and in her eyes, I was always doing something wrong or at the very least, not good enough, so I was without my phone more often than not. I was going to have to give *this* back, for sure. I pressed the button to turn it on, and it immediately started vibrating.

Now we are on the same network. Think of this as our own private hotline.

For the second time in an hour, Rosheon had made me gasp. He'd thought of everything. Even though I had no idea how in the world I would explain it, I was flattered. He knew I would get it trouble if I went over my minutes, so he took care of that, too. What high school boy could roll like that?

FIVE

Dana

I didn't necessarily like doing the work, but I loved going to school. The world was just what you had to work so they let you keep coming back. High school fascinated me. It was its own little society. Everyone had a place, and mine was at the top.

Normally, the fun started before I even reached the building, as I walked up the long hill that led to the main building of Hillcrest High. Today was no different. This was the nice time of year, not quite hot yet, but warm enough where you really didn't have to wear a jacket. Spring was my favorite time, because in the winter, no one hung outside the school like this, so the fashion parade didn't happen.

Many of the early birds were already here, hanging out, perched in places that gave them a good view of whoever approached. Not wanting to disappoint my peeps, I made sure I was appropriately dressed every day. I started my strut as soon as I reached the corner and allowed enough time for me to take it slow.

As usual, people tried to holla at me as I passed. I just nodded and kept on going though. Not one of these knuckleheads out here was worth my time. I had my sights set on the better half of a set of twins. Everything else was just a distraction. A senior said something to me that I missed. I was just about to pass him when I heard him say, "You think you're too good to talk to me?"

I just smiled, because I was. And I had no time to be fooling around with any of these people who obviously were going nowhere. In my head, I was already taken.

I usually met Damika at school just a little early, and I couldn't wait to see her. That girl at church had presented me with a challenge, and I wanted to know what Damika thought. When the two of us put our heads together, we were something else. I didn't have time to fill her in on all of the details, but I already knew that she would be part of my plan. She was my best friend, my BFF as the corny people say.

Damika was in our usual spot. There were lots of people around, but no one was talking to her. I wasn't surprised and she didn't seem to care. She never had. I was pretty amazed by the way she came to school every day, bare-faced with no makeup, looking like she just threw on the first clothes that she touched, and somehow, it all worked. She got out of bed twenty minutes before she planned to leave the house and managed to get to school on time and not naked. It would take me a good hour to get it all together. Being fabulous wasn't easy. In the words of Kimora Lee, fabulosity takes some work.

Damika was pecking away at her phone so furiously she didn't even see me come up. I stood there for a minute before interrupting her.

"Hello," I said. "I'm here."

"Oh. Hi."

Wait a minute. "Really, that's all I get? And did you get a new phone? Don't tell me The Warden caved and decided to bring you into the twenty-first century."

"Yup, new phone. But there's no need for you to hate." My friend grinned ear to ear. Her smile was the best part of her. She just didn't know the power she had in that smile. At that moment, all of her great shined through. I just didn't understand why other people didn't see it. This was the Damika that other people needed to get to know.

Everyone wanted one of those new phones. They were the latest and greatest. I would normally get new gear before Damika did. The order of the universe had been disturbed.

"I saw that commercial on TV. It was hot! I wish my mother would hook me up."

"You know it." She went right back to texting.

I narrowed my eyes. "Well, what good thing did you do? Or did your mother get abducted by aliens and replaced with a generous being who believes that you deserve all the technology - and clothes? Will the alien buy you new clothes now, too and can you get some for me?" I really tried not to pout, but it was hard.

At this point, I expected to hear a story about how she was surprised, anything. Instead, Damika just shrugged. "You know." That was it.

Huh? I needed more info. But from the serious way Damika pecked at her phone, it was obvious that I wasn't going to get any. Right here was where we differed. I would be all ecstatic about my phone, taking pictures, trying out every feature. Even holding it so that people could see me with it, but not her. Damika never got excited about anything. She was always poker-faced and cool as could be. Nothing moved her. No pride. No bragging. Damika was a goody-two-shoes to the bone.

And that's where I'd come in. She needed some excitement in her life. Maybe one of the twins could provide that excitement. The two of us were going to have an adventure, but I had to get to work. I had to whip her into adventure-shape before next Sunday. I was going to give Damika a make-over. She would be so hot when I got done that BOTH of the twins would be sweating her. Well, maybe not.

"Are you still going with me, Sunday?" I was real curious about who she was texting, but didn't ask. As far as I knew, I was her only close friend.

She didn't look up, but nodded.

"Good. We have some work to do. I've decided that we are going to be so fabulous when we walk up in there, everyone, not just those cute twins, is going to have to pay attention. To us both."

"You do know that this is church, not a video shoot, right? My mother isn't going to let us go out nowhere looking like we are going to a nightclub."

Of course I knew that. "Don't worry. They aren't ready for us yet. And when I'm done dressing you. . ."

Damika sighed heavily. "I never agreed to that. And my mother isn't going to let me go shopping."

I knew that, too. "I will handle that. Just meet me after school so we can put our heads together. The usual spot."

SIX
Damika

The day went by in a blur. For some reason, it was like I was in a daze and I couldn't stop day-dreaming. I couldn't concentrate on anything that any of my teachers were saying, not even in science, and that was usually my favorite class. Instead, I kept playing with that little shoe around my neck. My mother had almost seen it, too; I'd taken it off to take a shower and she'd come into my room. Thank goodness I'd thrown my shirt on top of it. I almost jumped out of my skin when she started to pick up my clothes.

"I told you about leaving your clothes on the floor, Damika." She'd bent down to scoop of the little pile of clothes at the foot of my bed.

"I got it, Mommy." I cringed as soon as the words left my mouth. I'd said that with just a little too much force. I tried to cover it up with a smile as I snatched the clothes from under my mother's fingertips, half waiting for her to give me one of her famous backhands that she was so proud of.

She didn't. Instead she raised one of her finely sculptured eyebrows and stood there with her hands propped on her hips and gave me her famous look that said I was treading on thin ice. Thank goodness that I'd been out of her reach with furniture in between us.

The bell couldn't ring fast enough. I wasn't sure I could take another minute of the torture that was school. The teacher had been talking at me for what seemed like an eternity and his words kept hitting my brain and bouncing off. Days like this were a waste. I would have gotten more out of staying home and sleeping.

As soon as the bell sounded, I moved like someone put a fire under me. I grabbed my stuff and rushed out to the front of the school where I was supposed to meet Dana. Her and her plans. She'd somehow gotten it into her head that I needed re-making in order to go to church with her. If anything, I *knew* how to do church and could give her a few lessons. I had plenty of church-girl dresses ready and waiting and really didn't need her help, although she surely wouldn't be feeling anything I chose. I refused to be defined by my clothes. I loved Dana like she was my sister, but she was far more superficial than I cared to be.

I pushed through the crowd as best I could. The usual suspects were in the usual places. The posers and the potheads all held down their respective spots. The stupid boys that raked you with their eyes as you passed, check. The boys who didn't date black girls, check. The smart Asians, check. The trendy Asians that looked like harajuku threw up on them, check. The cheerleader types trying to be seen, check. Everyone was in the same place they were everyday, as if someone had turned a camera on them and yelled "action" when the bell rang. Dana loved this mess, but I hated it. Most days, I just wanted to get through the mob of people and away from the school.

Our school was really some kind of weird social experiment, I was convinced of this. At one time, it was the place to go in Queens if you were into science or art, but now it was the most dangerous school in the area, its only claim to fame as that Fran Drescher, went there. My mother reminded me of this every time she watched her reruns of that show The *Nanny* on Nick at Night.

Dana and I usually met all the way at the bottom of the two flights of huge stone steps in front of our school, that way, we could take everything in, and there was always something going on. I tried to spot her from the top of the steps, but she was nowhere in sight. She was going to torture me today and leave me out her with all these plastic people. Normally, she would be there before me, but today, she was ghost.

Just as I made it to our spot, my phone buzzed. Not the regular phone, but the new one Rosheon had given me. I flipped it open as my eyes searched the crowd for Dana. I'd thought that the necklace was the best part of the gift, but

I think the phone definitely was. Before, I wouldn't have been able to talk to Rosheon at all until I could get to my computer, and only then if my mother wasn't around.

"Got a minute?" The deepness of Rosheon's voice always made me smile.

"Just barely. I'm meeting my girl." Even though I was outside, I whispered like I was sitting next to my mother in the first pew.

"Why don't you text her and tell her you'll catch up with her later. I need you to hang with me for a bit."

I inhaled deeply and then looked up. I was hearing Rosheon in stereo. What in the world was he doing here? I loved being with him, but in person, in public, he made me just a little nervous. We had so much to talk about when we talked online, but his appearance reminded me how much older than me he really was. I snapped the phone closed as he walked toward me.

As usual, my man was fine. He wore a crisp, blue button down shirt that he let stay outside his pants. His jeans were looking good, too. Not too big so they would be falling down, but just big enough to show he had it going on but could still look neat. Like he had a job, as my mother would say.

"Hey, you." I grinned anyway. "Me and my girl always go home together. What kind of friend would I be if I ducked out?" I glanced around nervously, suddenly aware that Rosheon looked more like a teacher than a student.

"You'd be a grown ass woman." Rosheon leaned into my ear and smelled me, his voice was barely above a growl as he spoke.

I sucked in my breath. It made no sense at all for him to be able to just take my breath away like he could. When he inhaled, all of my air went with him. *A grown ass woman.* It made me weak that he thought of me like that. I was so used to people telling me what I couldn't do because of my age, but for Rosheon, age really was nothing but a number. I swallowed hard. My decision was made for me, just like that. Dana would understand. I shot her a short text message, slipped my hand into his large one and followed Rosheon to his car.

"What did you have in mind?" I tried to keep a straight face as I sat there, but I wanted to grin ear to ear. My mother was always telling me that I was a kid and treating me like I couldn't make decisions for myself. It was like she was smothering me sometimes. I had a good head on my shoulders, and most of the time I did okay. I stayed out of trouble (at least trouble that she knows about) and I got reasonably good grades. A little breathing room would be good. As it was, she wasn't expecting me home until six, so I had a few hours, otherwise, she would have been blowing up my phone already, asking me when I'd be getting home.

Rosheon didn't answer me. He just smiled and pulled away from the school. My stomach did a little flip. We'd been hanging out some, but truth be told, we hadn't been anywhere other than Starbucks together, and even then, I'd met him there. I'd sat in his car a few times, but had never let him actually take me anywhere before.

"You trying to surprise me?" I blushed.

Rosheon put his hand on my knee and nodded. How could I not trust him? I would just have to wait and see what he had up his sleeves. He was so full of surprises lately, but I had yet to be disappointed.

SEVEN
Dana

Me and the church boy talked on the phone all week. I'd only seen him one time and I had to admit I was starting to feel him. He was just so easy to talk to, it was amazing. Every break, there was a new text on my phone from him.

I can't stop thinking about you.

Or

Two days until Sunday.

Every message I read like that made my heart skip a beat. I tried really hard to follow the rules. Everyone knew that you couldn't text back too fast, because then you'd look too thirsty. If you took too long then you looked like you didn't care. Neither one was good. I waited a full twenty minutes before I replied to him, or at least I tried to. If you'd a told me it would be like this, I would have never believed it. I almost didn't go to church that day, now here I was, sprung, risking getting in trouble for using my phone in school, and heaven knows I didn't want that. They would take my phone if I was caught using it during school hours and my mother would have to come up to the school to get it back. That would be worse. My mother wasn't as bad as Damika's, but she'd probably still lose her mind. I'd probably lose my phone privileges altogether if that happened. Still, I couldn't help myself.

After the bell rung, I stopped at my locker and called him. I couldn't wait any longer.

"You're still coming on Sunday, right?" He sounded as excited as I felt.

"That's the plan." I sunk into the chair near my locker. "You sure you don't have a girlfriend?" He'd told me he didn't before, but that was just too good to be true. As fine as he was, there had to be a woman in the woodwork somewhere, especially the way that one girl was trippin' when she met me last week.

"Naw," he said, "my brother is the one that's more the ladies man, not me. I'm the quiet one. I usually don't have time for all that."

"Usually?"

"You're the exception. When I saw you, I knew I had to just stop everything I was doing and just pay attention."

I wanted to believe him, even though that girl was all up in my face the day we'd met. Michelle, or whatever her name was, had been guarding him like a pit bull in a junkyard. I still blushed though. I couldn't help it. It'd been a long time since I felt like this, maybe never. He might live far, but we were really getting to know each other and I liked what I was seeing. I started to answer him, but my phone beeped, telling me that a text had come in.

"I want you to sing with us."

"I never said I sang. What are you talking about?"

"The Choir. In the Amen Chorus." The teen choir had its own name and performed separately from the big choir. They were almost as good, too. "I told you I'm the director. And everybody sings."

I wasn't really trying to be a singer, but I knew I sounded good, at least I did in the shower. I was no Mariah Carey, but I'd had my share of solos. "But don't you have to be a member for that? I don't know how many times I'll be able to come to your church."

"You let me worry about that. And they only sing once a month anyway. I just want you near me on Sunday, that's all. You've seen how big the church is. Would you rather be sitting near me, or way off somewhere in the back of the third balcony?"

I chuckled. It was a little funny to be talking about a third balcony in a church, and if I hadn't been there, I wouldn't believe it. I glanced at the clock above me. Just then, I noticed how empty the halls were. We'd been talking longer than I realized.

"I gotta go. I was supposed to meet Damika fifteen minutes ago," I said. She was probably standing outside, calling me all sorts of names by now. "I'm going to have to talk to you later."

"Promise?"

My stomach flip-flopped. "Absolutely."

"You'll think about singing?"

"We'll see. I'll call you around nine, as usual."

From the way we sounded, you would think we'd been talking a few months instead of a week. It felt so good, though. I felt like I'd known him forever. We'd only talked on the phone, but I was already on my way to sprung. I wasn't going to make him any promises. I knew that I didn't need to be embarrassing myself trying to sing, but it might not be a bad idea. I could lip sync if they were real good. There were so many people in that choir, no one would be able to tell anyway. My mother might not trip so much if I was in the choir. She might actually like it.

I couldn't' hold back the grin on my face as I ran outside to meet Damika. It was only about twenty minutes after dismissal, and the front of the school had just about cleared already. I almost skipped down the step to out meeting spot, but stopped dead in my tracks as I got closer to where we usually hooked up. Damika wasn't there. I expected her to be there like she had been before, pecking away on her new phone. I was convinced that she'd found a new way to show off her toy.

I didn't see her anywhere near, either. There were still a few stragglers. I asked around, but didn't get much of a response. Most of the stragglers had nowhere to go and no purpose and looked at me as if I was speaking alien when I questioned them. For a second, I was confused, and then I remembered her text. Damika had sent me a text when I was on the phone with Jeffrey. I scrambled to pull up my text messages.

Something came up?

What in the world? I was almost offended. What could have come up that was more important than me? This was unlike Damika. How was I supposed to do her makeover if she wasn't with me? I started toward home, but texted her back. She was going to have some explaining to do for this one.

EIGHT
Damika

Rosheon drove into Flushing, away from the direction I lived in. I was dying to ask him where we were going, but could tell that he wanted to surprise me, so I didn't ask too many questions. I didn't want him to re-think the idea of me as a woman, instead of some kid who couldn't be patient.

I sank into his plush seat covers and enjoyed Mary J. Blige, resisting the urge to sing along, even though I was really feeling what she was sinking. *Mr. Wrong.* My mother loved that song. If Rosheon was wrong for me, the way I knew my mother and Dana would say he was, this sure felt good.

Every few minutes, Rosheon squeezed my thigh. He kept his hand on my leg for the entire ride. It made me uncomfortable at first, but I started to get used to it after a few blocks, even though the sweat from his palm was making my leg damp. He was obviously more comfortable with me than I was with him, but I wasn't going to worry about it.

"What time do you have to be home?" he asked.

"My mother isn't expecting me for a minute." His question made me even more curious, and just when I thought I couldn't take it anymore, he stopped.

"You ready?"

My stomach turned flips. "I'm not sure. What should I be ready for?" Although I was enjoying being surprised, the hairs on the back of my neck prickled.

Rosheon's face got serious and he looked at me with those big eyes of his. I never noticed how long his eyelashes were before. "You trust me?"

I hesitated. Nothing good ever came after that question. The last time someone asked me that, I'd almost had a major accident on a killer hill on my skates. I think I'd been traumatized for life and I know I haven't been on my skates since then, and that was four years ago. Still, Rosheon gave me so many good feelings, I was sure it was fine.

"C'mon. I'll be good, I promise." Rosheon leaned over and brushed my cheek with his soft lips. I gasped and touched my face where his lips had been. I needed no more convincing than that. He got out of the car and came around to my side, opening the door for me.

He took my hand as I got out and we walked around the corner, hand in hand. There were only a few people around and Queens Boulevard was packed as usual. Rosheon didn't even hesitate, and I tried not to panic as I realized where we were. I'd driven past this place in my mother's car. I was in front of the Kew Motor Inn.

I'd never been there before, but everyone knew about it. The Kew was the famous spot where seniors went on prom night, after everything was over. This was where girls went when they were ready to give up the goods, which I was not. My head swam as we walked through the door. I slowed down, but Rosheon guided me firmly.

He didn't stop at the desk, but my eyes fixed on a sign right in front. Hourly rates. *$80.00 for four hours.* Hourly. What was he thinking? I swallowed heavily.

"You okay?" he asked.

I shook my head. "Why are we here?" I barely managed to get the words out. I liked Rosheon and all that, but I wasn't ready for this. My mother would kill me if she knew I'd even walked in front of this place.

"I thought we could just spend some time alone." He paused. "We don't have to do anything and if you don't want to, let me know and it's all good. I'll take you home."

Every bone in my body told me I should just leave right then, and I wanted to, but for some reason it was as if someone had painted the bottom of my feet with Super Glue. I was rooted to the spot. He must have thought I was born yesterday. Yeah, I was young, but I was not *that* young. How could I have let this happen? What was worse was that nobody knew where I was, not even Dana.

Rosheon rubbed my arm and then made his way to the front desk. I stood in the same spot, frozen, looking back and forth from Rosheon to the door, trying to figure out what I was going to do. I could see no way to exit, at least not one that wouldn't leave me looking like a scared little baby. I wasn't ready to take this step with Rosheon, but I didn't want him to think I was too young for him either. He looked up at me and smiled as he stood by the counter, and just then, my phone rang. Not the one that Rosheon had given me, but the other one. I reached into my pocket and took it out, glancing at the screen.

It was my mother. *Thank you, God!* Instead of being scared out of my wits, relief flooded over me. I didn't have to make a decision, my mother had just made it for me. She had some sense of timing. I flipped open the phone and a grin spread over my face. "Hey, Mom, how are you?"

We chatted for a minute. Rosheon came back over and waited patiently. "Yes, I can do that. I'll be a little late though, I had to go to the central library on the way home. That's where I am now, on Queen's boulevard."

It was only half a lie, really. I *was* on Queen's Boulevard, after all. My mother had some kind of radar. I was just so happy to hear from her. "Okay," I said, I'll be there soon."

Rosheon had a look of disappointment on his face. "I already paid."

"I know, and I'm sorry. But my mother—"

He held up his hand to stop me. "You don't have to explain. I'll just take you home." He guided me toward the door.

I was glad he wasn't angry, but there was no way in hell I was getting back in his car. He had some nerve. If he wasn't so damned cute, I'd be furious.

"Don't worry about it. I can take the bus. My mother wants me to stop at the store and I know you live in the other direction anyway," I told him.

It's not that I thought he was a bad guy or anything like that. I just needed some time to think things through a bit.

"Are we okay?" he asked. Rosheon had a slight smile on his face and it made his half-dimple stand out even more. My stomach flip-flopped. He sure was fine. And he smelled good. Always.

I nodded. "We're fine. It's just that my mother—"

"You don't have to make excuses or explain to me. I can wait to spend time with you. I'm not going anywhere." Rosheon ran his finger lightly across my cheek. And I smiled. I had no idea why I'd been so scared. It was obvious he really cared about me and had my best interest in mind.

I was glad he'd cut me off, because the other half of that sentence was that my mother was going to beat my behind if she knew where I was. I let him walk me to the bus stop. Rosheon waited with me, but the mood was spoiled. I had no more butterflies in my stomach. Instead, I just felt weird and stupid, and Rosheon looked old. I'm sure he was thinking that I was a baby, but I didn't care. It wasn't my time yet, but I knew that he liked me and really was willing to wait.

NINE
Dana

My house was all crazy when I got there. The door was propped open and people were coming in and out, carrying things from up the block.

What in the world was going on?

As I got closer, I realized that there was a small U-Haul truck parked outside and the four men I saw weren't carrying things out, they were carrying them from the truck to the house. Dennis was outside talking to the men excitedly.

"Be careful with that", he yelled. He looked in my general direction, but he didn't even acknowledge me. No surprise there. The other night had clearly been a momentary lapse of sanity on his part. I pushed past the debris in the front yard and went to find my mother.

It didn't take long. She was in the front room, pushing a couch around, one that I did not recognize. She looked a hot mess, too. She had on grey, baggy, old-fashioned sweats, the kind with the elastic around the ankle. Mom sweats. They sagged in the butt, she had a black smudge on her left cheek, and her hair was real messy. If I didn't know better I'd think that she'd she had just gotten out of bed.

"What happened to our old couch?" I asked. It wasn't that old, actually, but it had been quite comfortable. I'd loved curling up on it to watch television on the weekends and sitting way too close to my mother when she let me. She would act like she didn't like it, but I know a part of her did.

"Dennis's is nicer. And newer." She nudged at a brown leather thing with her knees, obviously trying to push in into place.

"What?" There was no way that this hard, butt-ugly leather would be as comfortable as ours had been. The gold had worn off the studs that rimmed the funky-looking leather. It looked as if it had been rejected from a stone-age thrift shop. My father had bought our couch. I'd been with him when he'd picked it out. This one was straight (and not curved like ours had been) and hard looking, and the leather had these worn down studs all the way around the base.

"I didn't tell you? Dennis is moving in."

Her words didn't exactly register. "Moving in where?"

"Dana, don't give me attitude. Here. He's moving in here. I know I told you."

You would think that something so major would have to be discussed by all members of the household. "No, Mom, you didn't. Do you think that's a good idea? We don't know him that well, and I think my dad is going to be upset about it."

"Give me a hand. We don't, but I do. He's a good man. And you dad gets no damned say. He doesn't pay any of the bills up in here anymore."

I grabbed the end of the couch where she'd pointed, trying to choose my words carefully. "Does he even have a job? He's like Tommy on those *Martin* re-runs you always watch. We're not even sure what he does for a living."

My mother stood up and put her hands on her hips. I could tell by the look on her face that I'd gone too far. I cringed before she even opened her mouth.

"When did you become such a wise ass? I'll bet you don't ask your father those questions about his women friends, those one-night stand hoochies that he keeps introducing you to. I deserve just as much happiness as he does."

"But he's not moving any of them in-"

"I pay the bills here and you are still just a child. I suggest you take yourself to your room and out of my business before I treat you like a three-year-old and spank that smart behind of yours. I would think that you were smarter than to stand for that old double-standard, Dana. There is no reason in the world that it's okay for him and not for me. What's good for the goose is good for the gander, right?"

I counted to ten, and tried hard to hold my tongue. I truly didn't understand my mother. Why could she see nothing wrong with moving some man into the house? What ever happened to all her talk about "taking it slow" after daddy moved out? And hadn't I heard her say that I shouldn't even consider living with someone before I got married? Or did those rules not apply to her because she was old?

"Just go upstairs and do your homework. Now."

She went back to pushing at the ugly couch and I left her there, but not before I noticed something. She hadn't had a drink today. At least not yet.

TEN
Damika

My mother was in a good mood when I got home. She'd saved me and didn't even know it. I made sure that I'd gotten everything she needed at the grocery store, with no mistakes or variations.

"Do you have a lot of homework?" she asked. Mom was fully dressed, not like usual. Normally, the first thing she'd do when she got home would be to kick off her shoes and slide into some ugly, old lady sweats so she could relax. She didn't look at all like she was winding down. She didn't have on work clothes, but she still looked like she was ready for anything. She had on her nice jeans, the ones that didn't look like "mom jeans", instead these were kinda hot on her, low cut in the front but not in the back.

She was too cheery. It caught me off guard. I was immediately cautious; I felt like I was experiencing the calm before the storm.

"Not really," I said finally.

"You don't have to sound like you're in trouble. Put that stuff in the kitchen. We're going to the mall."

"Mom, are you sick?" Maybe I'd heard her incorrectly. We never went to the mall on a school night.

"No, Miss Smarty. I feel like I've been neglecting you lately, so I thought we'd have a little mid-week treat." She jingled her car keys. Treat is right. She almost ever let me do anything during the week that didn't have the word library or church in it.

I did as she asked, and then ran upstairs to change my clothes. The only thing I loved more than the mall was the mall with Dana, but my mother would do just fine, especially since she had a little cash in her bag. With Dana, we'd be just window-shopping. I changed my shoes and took off Rosheon's necklace and dropped it on the counter, then moved the mouse on the computer. There was a message from Rosheon waiting, just two lonely words. The words "I'm sorry" blinked at me from the chat window. I deleted the message and quickly changed my status menu on my IM to "out shopping" and headed back downstairs to join my mother. Rosheon obviously needed some cool down time. He could wait.

She was already in the car. I couldn't help but grin as I slid in beside her. We were at the mall in no time. It'd been so long since I'd been there during the week that the emptiness was strange for me. Everything was cool for about two stores, and then she started in.

"So, Damika."

I immediately tensed for whatever was coming next. I wasn't surprised, though. Spontaneous shopping wasn't free. There had to be some catch to it.

She continued. "Have you given any thought to what we talked about? College?"

I rolled my eyes. Truthfully, I hadn't. "I have time, Ma." I ran my finger across a bad, purple dress in front of me. We were in Macy's, in the baby Phat department. Kimora had really been stepping up her design game lately, and I was trying to ignore the phone in the bottom of my bag that was vibrating like crazy.

My mother grabbed my shoulder and spun me around. "No, you don't have time. I need you to take this seriously. We need to plan *now*. We have to think about everything you do leading to college, and that means what you will do this summer, too."

"Okay. Why?" Did she have to be so rough? My shoulder hurt where she'd grabbed me. "I'm only a sophomore."

My mother's face hardened. "Why? Because I'm busting my ass to make sure you get a good education that's why. Because I want better for you, that's why." She paused. "I never got to go to college until I could send myself." She lowered her voice. "I want better for you."

And just like that, her eyes welled up with tears. She knew how to lay it on, because I suddenly felt guilty.

"I gave my life away when I could have done better. I was so busy following behind your father, I barely made it through college and I was better than that."

"I'm sorry, Ma. I *have* been thinking about it some." By the time tears come, it was usually too late to fix things, but I tried anyway, then tried to steer us out of the store. My mother was making a scene and the clerk was staring at us. It was bad enough she'd been watching us like a hawk ever since we'd come in the door, but now she was seeing my mother break down, too.

"Think about it *more*. You need to think about it more." She was practically sobbing and her lips quivered. We stopped at a bench outside the store and sat down. "I should have gone to graduate school, but I didn't listen. By the time I looked up, it was too late. I was married with a family and we couldn't afford it. I can't let you make the same mistakes I did." She sniffled, then dug in her purse for a tissue.

"But you do okay, now, Mom. It's not like we're poor." I swallowed hard. What was I supposed to say to this? My mother was the one who comforted me when things got rough, it wasn't supposed to work the other way around. "We're happy."

"Okay isn't enough.' She closed up then. As quickly as she'd turned on the water works, she turned them off. "I guess we are happy." Her face became unreadable and she snapped her bag shut. "You just remember what I'm telling you. You get your education. And don't put your life or your dreams on hold for any man, okay? And if you have any doubts, you ask me first."

My shit felt small then, and I felt guilt, big time. Why in the world was I running around with Rosheon, and for what? What would hanging around with him get me? I pushed the thought to the back of my mind. He may have been moving a little fast, but I could slow him down. Rosheon was as crazy about me as I was about him. He wasn't trying to keep me from anything. My mother obviously had some unresolved issues with my father. He was dead, so she was going to have to work on that.

"Let's go, Damika. You have school tomorrow. Let's not talk about this again, okay? You just remember that nothing in life is free."

We didn't say much all the way back to the house. My stomach did backflips all the way home. It was almost like she could read my mind, but I knew I'd been careful. There was no way she could possible know about Rosheon. I kept thinking about my mother in tears and trying to figure out what she was really tripping about, and the close call I'd had earlier. I really didn't know Rosheon at all. The phone he'd had given me was stuck down in the bottom of my bag and it'd practically been going off non-stop since I'd left the house. I had to almost will myself not to jump every time it rang. Finally, I slid my bag down on the floor of the car so I wouldn't feel it and be forced to explain to my mother why I couldn't sit still. She was going to find out about him sooner or later, but the way she'd broken into tears in the mall let me know that it'd better be way, way later.

I had no time to contemplate my mother's mood swings and didn't want to. I left her in the kitchen and ran upstairs to check my messages. I probably had about five hundred, and all of them would be from Rosheon for sure. I closed the bathroom door behind me just to make sure my mother wouldn't catch me.

Seven messages, all from Rosheon, in the space of a little over two hours. I listened to them all. He sure sounded pitiful. He wanted to see me again soon and apologized over and over, and by the time I was done listening, a big smile was on my face and I'd almost forgotten the weirdness with my mother in the store. I quickly sent him a text.

Busy this weekend. Going 2 church N Brooklyn w Dana.

My finger barely left the phone before I received a reply.

Don't do that. Hang out w me.

You know I can't. Means a lot 2 my friend. Might

Njoy it anyway.

I flushed the toilet for good measure, opened the door and ran dead smack into my mother. She was waiting for me, right outside the bathroom door.

"Ma," I said. "What in the world are you doing?"

Her arms were folded across her lips and her face was stone. A chill ran up my spine. How in the world could I have gotten in trouble that fast? We'd only just gotten home.

"I could ask you the same damn thing." She unfolded her arms and held up the necklace that Rosheon had given me. "You wanna tell me where this came from?"

My stomach sank. "I bought it?" I couldn't even convince myself.

She stood a step toward and I cringed. "Try again, Damika. With what money?"

"Allowance?"

"You're getting deeper in." I kept my eye on her hands as she paused and switched her weight from one hip to the other. "You can barely save enough money to get on the bus, much less buy something like this. I'm going to ask you this one more time. Where. Did. This. Come. From? And don't tell me from Dana because we can get her on the phone right now."

I dropped my head. How could I be so stupid? I should have put the dumb thing in a drawer. "Rosheon gave it to me."

All the air seemed to leave the room. "Rosheon? Who the hell is that? Does he go to school with you? I never heard of no Rosheon. You got a boyfriend, now?" She dropped her hands (finally) and paced my floor. "Didn't we just have this discussion? You know better than to take any gifts from any boys. Can't no boy buy something like this. What's he do for a living? He certainly ain't no student. Where's his people?" She finally stopped talking and glared at me so hard I swear she could see right through me.

I panicked. Just as she walked close to me, I reached out and tried to grab the necklace. "You shouldn't go through my things, Mom. This was private. It was in my room."

My mother got a crazed look in her eye. "Private? Ain't nothing up in my house private, girl. Everything in my house, belongs to me, including you. The clothes on your back, everything. You better step back before I slap the black off of you." By now, she was shrieking at the top of her lungs.

I shrunk back away from her. She was well past pissed when she talked about making me colorless. Why didn't I make sure that I was between her and the door? She was getting pretty close to her breaking point, and my mother could be real crazy when that happened. As it was, I had nowhere to run.

"This is my house. I pay the bills here. You don't have a thing, not one thing." She paused. "Didn't I just tell you that nothing is free? You're a smart girl, Damika. Too smart for this." She shook the necklace at me and I jumped. "I tell you what, Miss Thing. You and I are going to give this back. And I will pick you up from school from now on, like you're a six-year-old, because that is how you're acting. I can't trust you to go from there to here without taking gifts from some strange man."

"But, Ma-"

"Shut it." The look in her eye told me that I shouldn't say anything else. When she got like this, there was no explaining. She left and I fell across my bed and cried. She would never let me out of her sight again. With my mother on my back like a private detective, I'd be thirty before I got to see Rosheon or anyone else again. She might as well send me to a convent right now.

ELEVEN
Dana

Everyone in my house was acting like it was business as usual, even though our house had grown by one member. Dennis was creeping me out. He was always there in the morning when I woke up, and he barely mumbled a hello. By the time I got downstairs, he was sitting in the kitchen, doing nothing. He just sat there and it felt like he was watching me just too hard. I couldn't wait to get to school now for two reasons. First, each day got me closer to when I could go back to the church in Brooklyn with my dad, and second, if I was out of the house, I was away from do-nothing Dennis.

The last bell rang and I packed up my stuff to get outside and meet Damika as usual. I'd have to talk to Jeffrey later. Damika's mother had been driving her to school every day, and picking her up, too, like she was in middle school or something. This new man of hers was bad news. I hadn't met him yet and my girl was already in trouble. The good part for me was I got a ride home, too, even if I had to endure

Damika's sad face for the entire time. I might as well enjoy the perks. I wasn't the one in trouble.

She was already in our spot when I came down the steps. I slowed down as I got closer to her. Damika was talking to someone, a guy, and from the looks of things, it wasn't a great conversation. I'd never seen this person before, but there were a lot of kids I didn't know. Okay, not really, but there we certainly a few. I started to hang back and wait until they were done, but all of a sudden, he grabbed my girl by her arm and she was obviously not happy with that.

"Ow, Roshcon,' she whined. "You're hurting me."

Rosheon? So this as the mystery man. I strolled right up to them, surprised that Damika was letting him put his hands on her like he was.

"Hey, Damika, when's your mother coming?" I asked.

He let her go, and they locked eyes.

"Dana, this is Rosheon that I told you about."

I tried to play it off like it was all good. "Oh, so *this* is the mystery man?"

We all relaxed a little as Rosheon took a step back.

"Yes," Damika said. "I was just telling him about going to church with you and your father in Brooklyn."

"—And I'm guessing he's not too happy."

"I'm right here. You can ask me. No, I'm not, but I guess it's all good."

"It's church, Rosheon. Why wouldn't it be?" Damika had obviously found some courage now that I was here.

"Because you are going to meet some dude, that's why—"

"She's not. I am." She'd obviously shared too much. "Did you tell him you were grounded, too? You should have asked me for advice and I would have told you how to handle the Warden and your daddy."

Damika's mother's car pulled up beside us before she could answer and jumped from the car like it was on fire. Had she even put the thing in park?

"Who the hell is this?" Mrs. Woods immediately went into Angry Black Mother mode, complete with hand on her hip. Is this the boy?"

I was embarrassed for Damika. Her mother had come out swinging. If Rosheon knew what was good for him, he'd get away from here fast.

"Mrs. Woods," Rosheon said, cutting her off, "it's so nice to finally meet you. Your daughter didn't tell me how beautiful you were."

I smirked. This was going to be good. I know he didn't think she would fall for so obvious a line. Damika's mother looked at him like she thought he was crazy. "And you are?" she said. "It seems you have an advantage. My daughter hasn't told me too much about you at all. In fact, she told me nothing. I found out about you by mistake."

"Really? My name is Rosheon Edwards. I'm pleased to meet you." He held out his hand for a handshake like this was some business meeting or something. His smile was warm and big, though, as if I hadn't seen them arguing just a few minutes before. "I was just asking Damika for some directions."

There was an awkward pause as Damika's mother looked from Damika to Rosheon, and then finally to me. If a leaf fell off a tree at that point, I think we would have heard it. Finally, she accepted his offer for a handshake. I swear I could hear Damika exhale.

"Are you a student? You look kind of old to be hanging around here."

Damika interrupted. "No, Mom, he's not. He-"

"Graduated last year. A year early. I hope that's not a problem." Rosheon's dimple was so big it was practically winking at us. He really wasn't bad looking. Two points to Damika for that.

It didn't look like The Warden was buying it. Rosheon was easily twenty years old. Maybe more than that. He stepped forward and took Mrs. Woods's arm as if he were planning to take a stroll with an old friend on a boardwalk. Damika and I stood there with our mouths open in disbelief. Rosheon had no idea who he was messing with. Mrs. Woods might look all refined, but she would give him a beat down like she was a grown man in a minute. We'd all heard the stories. Supposedly she'd been quite the hellraiser in her day.

They walked away from us, arm and arm. We held our breath as we waited for all hell to break loose, only, it didn't. Instead Mrs. Woods threw her head back and laughed like a school girl. I alternated between looking at them and at Damika. This was getting real interesting. My girl's face went from butterscotch to green in no time at all. What in the world was going on?

"Mom?" she said. "Um…"

Had they forgotten about us? Or did Rosheon have some kind of plan? He was good, because what I imagined should be happening, wasn't. There was no cussing, no swearing. No one was cutting anyone else. Nothing.

"Get in the car, girls."

We looked at each other again, and I shrugged.

I slid into the car next to Damika, but I was as confused as she felt. "What do you think they're talking about?"

Her mother laughed again.

"I don't know. This isn't good."

I chuckled. "You got that right."

Damika concentrated on her mother's profile. "Is she flirting? It looks like my mother is flirting. He's half her age."

"And almost twice yours. You didn't tell me he was so much older."

"He's not twice my age. And I did tell you."

TWELVE
Damika

I was grounded, plain and simple. My mother dropped me at school and was there like clockwork to pick me up. There were positives to this. I didn't have to take the bus, but that was also a negative, especially on beautiful days like today.

The sun was shining and there was just a light breeze when I got out of school. It would have been a great day to take my time getting home, but I didn't dare risk pissing off my mother even more. I came right outside to where I normally met Dana, and my mother wasn't there yet like I'd thought she'd be. Rosheon was waiting, though, and before I could get rid of him, both Dana and my mother rolled up on us.

Dana surprised us right in the middle of our argument and she was giving me grief and putting her nose where it didn't belong. Rosheon really wasn't her business. By the time my mother showed up, I was in trouble for sure, but Rosheon surprised me by charming my mother just a little too much. Damika and I watched in disbelief as she laughed and cheesed with Rosheon like she wasn't pissed off just a few minutes before. By the time she was done with their conversation, and started walking back to the car, she was all smiles.

She put her hand on the door handle.

"If you say a word to my mother I'm not going with you to Brooklyn. Believe that." Dana thought she was the only one who could play hardball, but I'd learned from the best. We'd hung out together for years. I knew exactly what to say so she would leave me alone about Rosheon. I didn't need her approval for anything I did.

My mother hopped in the car, obviously happier than she'd been before she'd started flirting with *my* boyfriend. It seemed like her walk back the half of a block she'd covered arm in arm with Rosheon took forever. The few feet of sidewalk seemed to stretch out into something like a mile, as if we were under the influence of those Alice in Wonderland mushrooms. I braced myself for one of my mother's long lectures, but instead I got nothing. She put the car in gear and checked her mirrors, just like normal.

Dana and I looked at each other, all wide-eyed. She was surprised, too. She was probably counting on my mother to put me in my place or something. I tried to see my mother's face in the rearview mirror.

I held my breath and my tongue until she'd pulled away from the curb. "Mom," I said, "is everything okay?"

She glanced at me in the mirror. "Yes, of course. Rosheon seems like a nice young man."

"Excuse me?" Had he slipped her some drugs while she wasn't looking? Who was this woman and what had been done with my mother?

"He does seem a little old for you, and I still think you're too young to be dating, but if you had to have some secret crush, he doesn't seem like he's too bad of a choice. Besides, I don't think much harm can come of you telling him where the nearest Starbucks is, although I'm sure he didn't need to come all the way out of his way to get that information from you."

"I know, right? I bet he could have looked that up on his phone." Dana smirked.

I glared at her. She could keep her peanut gallery comments to herself. This was not a crush. Crushes happened to seven and eight year olds. As usual, my mother was treating me like I was a kid. Still, I couldn't' believe what I was hearing. Was she feeling okay? I stammered. "What did you talk about?"

"Nothing, really. Where he was from. His people. How you met."

I almost choked. "How we met?"

"Yes, he told me you met in that restaurant you kids go to for lunch, but I don't want you to think you have to keep secrets from me like this. It would've been so much better if we'd talked about it. Maybe then you wouldn't have thought that you had to hide things from me, and I do know a thing or two about men, you know."

I sat back in my seat. That was quick thinking. My mother knew that we all went to the place across the street at least once a week. If she knew we'd met on line, I'd be on tech lock down for sure. My mother didn't play when it came to some things. I wouldn't put it past her to turn off the electricity in *just* my room, take my computer indefinitely, and confiscate my phone. Both of them.

"Does this mean that she is off punishment, Mrs. Woods?"

I thought Dana was on my side, but she still had a scowl on her face. She wasn't buying any of it, not even a little, but she didn't understand Rosheon the way I did at all.

"Most certainly not. And you will give him back that necklace. You still can't accept it."

Now that was the mother I knew. Rosheon had been all polite and nice, and some of the stuff he'd said had kept me out of even more trouble. He might have thought he'd charmed my mother, but I knew the real deal. He'd just kept himself from getting an old-fashioned beat down.

THIRTEEN
Dana

When people start talking about the weather you know that stuff is messed up. I was surprised at Damika for threatening me the way she had after the Rosheon incident, but we didn't talk about it again. We'd get to that later. I still needed her to go with me to the church.

I'd waited all week for Sunday and had woken up early. I called Damika first thing.

"You're still going with me, right?"

She hesitated. "I guess."

"What's the problem? You promised. And I told you before, you won't regret it." I spelled it out for her again. "T-W-I-N-S. Don't tell me your mother is tripping? You did tell her it was church, right?" Damika's mother was the biggest church lady I knew.

"Well, I'm still sort of grounded, but you know Rosheon wasn't happy."

Did I hear her correctly? "Really, Damika?" That caught me off guard. "You barely know him, and since when do you let a man dictate what you do?"

Damika's breath was loud over the phone. "You know what, Dana? I never realized you were such a hater. You act like I'm not cute enough to have anyone interested in me. Not everyone likes girls like you, Dana."

What was she talking about? "What's that supposed to mean? Girls like me?"

She paused. "You know exactly what I mean. Cute, skinny girls, with all new clothes and makeup. Popular chicks. Just because I pay more attention to my grades than to clothes doesn't mean someone can't want to get with me."

My face stung as if she'd slapped me. What was she talking about? Is that what she thought of me?

"I never said that, Damika. It's just that we're supposed to be best friends, and if I hadn't seen the phone, you would never have mentioned it to me at all. I never see you with anyone, and as far as I knew, The Warden wasn't about to let you date."

"I didn't mention him to you because I didn't want anyone to know yet. I tried to tell you when I met him, but you tripped about the idea of meeting people online. It's not a big deal. Everyone does it. And you know how you can't keep a secret."

My eyes welled up with tears. "When was the last time I told anything you wanted kept secret? You know I got you, right?" I couldn't believe we were arguing over a guy. I swatted away my tears.

"Let me think-"

"Never mind. Stop tripping and tell me what's up."

Damika was strangely silent, almost like she'd hung up.

"Hello," I said. "You there?"

"He's older."

"Tell me something I don't know. College?"

"Not exactly."

Not Exactly? "Older than that?"

She paused again. "No, he didn't go."

"What does he do?"

"I don't know. He works. Stop with the questions. This ain't 'Jeopardy'."

Still, I had to pick up my face. A secret much-older man.

"Fine. Your secret, older, mystery man with no job doesn't own you, you know. You're sixteen, not married, and even then, women are not attached to their husbands at the hip nowadays. Eve came from Adam's rib, *outside* of his chest."

"So glad you have jokes," Damika said. "He's just trippin'. I'll be over in ten minutes."

I hung up the phone and hopped out of bed. So, Damika had a few tricks up her sleeve. I wondered what was so special about this Rosheon that she felt she had to hide him. Now I knew. Her mother would trip over any boyfriend at all, but an older one would surely get Damika grounded for the rest of her natural life. No wonder she'd been so secretive. We'd certainly have some time to talk about it today.

Unlike last time, I was prepared. I stood in front of my closet and carefully contemplated both of the outfits that I'd picked out the night before. I'd just thrown on any old thing last week, but this week, I wanted to look hot, but not heathen. Sexy, but not skanky. I finally decided on a bad chocolate wrap dress and shoes that I'd bought from BeBe.

I slipped them on, then admired the end result in the mirror. Sophisticated, or at least as sophisticated, yet still appropriate. I was ready. I hoped that Damika was just as prepared. I'd never gotten the chance to help her pick out her outfit like I'd wanted to, so I was a little worried.

Damika rang the doorbell right when she said she would. I wanted to talk to her more about Rosheon but didn't have the time. My father drove up before she even had a chance to step inside the house. We shouted goodbye to my mother, then both Damika and I slid into the backseat together.

"One of you could have sat up here. I'm not a chauffeur." He looked at me through the rearview mirror. As usual, my dad smelled good.

"I was trying to leave room for Wanda and I didn't want Damika to sit back hear by herself," I said. The truth was, I thought that maybe she would tell me more about her mystery older man.

I couldn't wait for him to turn on the music. As soon as he did, I turned to stare at Damika.

"So?"

She grinned and turned to look out of the window. "So, what?"

"You know you gotta tell me more. You can't leave me hanging. What's he like? Where'd you meet? Is he trying to get you to-"

She cut me off in mid-sentence. "Dana, your father."

"I know you're not shushing me."

Before I could get on her about being so secretive, her phone buzzed. She pulled it out of her purse, looked at it, then sent a text message. I didn't say a word while I waited for her to finish, although curiosity was killing me. I'd been patient before, but it was time for her to spill it about this new phone.

She grinned, shaking her head. "Don't ask." She paused and lowered her voice. "It was a gift."

"But you already had a phone—" And then it hit me. My mouth dropped open. He'd given it to her. She hadn't said that. "Oh." First the necklace that her mother mentioned, now this. This was serious. "I knew something was up when I saw it at school." I paused. Damika's mother barely thought that either one of us needed a phone at all, much less a brand new one with all the bells and whistles. Damika was a smart girl.

"Nothing is free," I said. I hated to admit I was starting to sound like the grown-up between us. Usually, that was

Damika's role. Now, I was sort of mad that she hadn't told me about this. "Are you-"

She raised her eyebrows, and I knew that she wasn't going to talk about it. We'd made a pact a long time ago about things like this. Whoever had sex first, we'd tell the other one. Damika hid this secret man for who knows how long, what else was she hiding? She'd hid her secret phone and her secret necklace. If you didn't tell your best friend things, who could you tell? My feelings were hurt. I wouldn't do her that way.

"You know you ain't right. You tell me everything."

She grinned. "Stop playing. I'm still the same me."

I narrowed my eyes. "I hope so. I kinda liked you the way you were."

We didn't talk much the rest of the way to the church. I stared out of the window for most of the ride, and every time I glanced over at Damika, She was pecking away on that stupid phone with a silly grin on her face. "Can you have a conversation with the people right here in front of you?"

"You're just hatin' because you don't have all this technology over there." She caught a glimpse of the scowl on my face. "I'm kidding. Just let me just finish this one note."

"You know it looks desperate if you answer them back too fast."

She finally put the phone in her purse. "There."

"Whatever." Damika had managed to ruin my morning and it hadn't even really gotten started. We were supposed to be strategizing and instead, she was communicating with her secret boyfriend.

I was annoyed with her, but as soon as I stepped out of the car, it was as good as forgotten. What if Jeffrey didn't like me after all? I would have jumped through all kinds of hoops for nothing, from convincing my mother, to acting all silly over him. I didn't want to end up with egg on my face.

"You didn't tell me it was a mega church." Damika slipped her arm in mine and we approached the building together.

I was glad she was with me, secrets and all. Her presence gave me strength, especially now that I knew she had a boyfriend. I mean, I talked a real good game, and sure, I got lots of attention at school, but I'd never *really* had a boyfriend. Now Damika had done something that I hadn't. I was supposed to be making her over, but maybe there was a thing or two that she could teach me. An older man. I was almost impressed.

"I didn't think it would matter."

"This is the original mega church." My father chimed in. "It was big like this when I was a kid."

"Wow, Dad. That was ages ago."

We all laughed, but I really didn't know what to do next. I was too afraid to admit it though. Right before we'd pulled up, I'd texted Jeffrey and he hadn't answered me yet. I really didn't know him that well and had only seen him once. Sure, we'd talked on the phone a trillion times since last week, but dudes would tell you anything in a text message. And how in the world was I going to find him in all these people? I didn't want to end up back in the balcony with my father again. Just as we hit the steps, a message came through.

Meet me in the choir room,.

A grin spread across my face. Now we were talking.

"Dad, I'm going down to the choir room." the words tumbled from my mouth so quickly I almost tripped over my own tongue. "I'll see you after okay?" A look of surprise spread across his face, but we took off before he could ask any questions. I knew I'd get drilled later, but hopefully, it would be worth it.

Damika and I found the choir room without too much trouble. The halls were full of people, but no one stopped us or asked where we were headed. Everyone seemed to be on a mission, and they all pretty much ignored us. For such a large building, it really wasn't that difficult to find my way, but I was sure it had its share of secrets.

The door to the choir room was an old, worn-looking brown door with a small window in it. The finish had worn off of the used-to-be-gold handle. I paused outside the room, smoothed my dress, wet my lips, took a deep breath and pushed the door open.

"You're sure going through a lot of trouble," Damika said. "These boys better be worth it."

"I promise you, your time will not wasted."

"Okay, this isn't for me. I got a man, remember?"

"Whatever," I said. "Now you're the one with jokes. Let's go."

Damika didn't try very hard to conceal her smirk. She raised her eyebrows like she didn't believe me, but she'd come this far. She tumbled into the room right behind me.

Like last time, it was swarming with people getting into and out of robes. I couldn't see Jeffrey at first, if he was in the room at all he was surely swallowed up in the sea of purple in front of me. A sinking feeling hit the pit of my stomach. Maybe this hadn't been such a good idea. I searched the crowd, but couldn't find him. What if I really didn't remember what he looked like? Just when I was about to give up, I felt a hand on my arm. I spun around and almost walked right into Jeffrey. Or at least I thought it was him.

"Jeffrey?"

"No James. Jeffrey's over there." He pointed toward the piano in the corner. It was surrounded by a swarm of people. I was confused for a moment, then realized that James was really James. He was missing the small mole on his face that Jeffrey had. If nothing else, I remembered that. I'd noticed it last week, when they were standing next to each other. It was funny how when they were together, the differences were obvious, but apart, not so much. I started in that direction and Damika stopped me, tugging on my arm.

"Hi, I'm Damika," she said. She'd turned back around and was standing in front of James. My girl was all smiles. You would have no idea that she was telling me how her man didn't want her to come just a little over a half hour ago.

"Oh, yeah. This is my best friend, Damika," I threw in even though she'd made her own introduction. I left Damika making moon eyes at James and made my way through all the people over to the piano.

He didn't see me coming. Jeffrey was sitting down, playing the piano and three girls were huddled around him. I stood just behind them and watched them warm up. He hit a key and they tried to hit the note, then faded out. I cleared my throat in the sliver of silence and he looked up.

"Dana. I'm glad you could come," he said. "Everybody, this is Dana. She's going to be joining us."

None of the three girls said hello. Only one of them nodded. A shiver ran up my spine. If I didn't know better, I would think that I wasn't too welcome. And why wasn't I getting more than a hello? He was treating me like I was just any old girl in the choir, and not someone that he'd talked to and texted almost non-stop for an entire week, making all kinds of suggestions about what I could expect when we saw each other again.

One of them cleared her throat. "Is *Michelle* coming today?" She practically spat out the name. I caught a flash of gold as she was talking. A grille on a girl. Ugh.

"I don't know. I haven't spoken to her since last week's practice. Come on," Jeffrey said to me. He squashed her hate pretty well. "We only have a few minutes. You read music, right?" Jeffrey shoved some sheet music into my hands so fast I almost dropped it. "Dana, just follow along as best you can. Don't sing what you don't know." He sat down and immediately started hitting the keys. He didn't so much as give me a sideways glance. I bit my lip. I know he didn't have me come all this way just to sing. I slid up next to the other girls so we could see the music better, but my heart wasn't in it. What kind of a welcome was that and where in the world had Damika disappeared to? As far as I could tell, she was nowhere in sight.

"Dana, you didn't tell me you could blow like that," Jeffrey said when we'd finished.

I blushed.

"I'll tell you what. Michelle isn't here and it looks like she isn't coming, so why don't you sing her solo?"

The other girls all spoke at once. "What?"

"I don't know–"

"It's all good," he said. "You'll be like our guest soloist. Here's the music. It's only a few lines and its nothing too difficult. We'll go over this and then we have to get into the choir stand or they are going to have my head."

The other girls grabbed their robes and slipped them on. They stared daggers at me without speaking, but one of them finally said, "So, she's just gonna go out there like that?" She pointed at my outfit.

"I almost forgot," Jeffrey said. "Give her Michelle's."

They stared at Jeffrey like he'd just told them to jump off a building.

"Well, it's not like she's coming. Give it to her." Jeffrey might have only been seventeen, but just then, he sounded like the school principal or something.

They weren't happy, but finally, the girl who had everything to say reached into the small closet near where we were standing and grabbed a robe and practically threw it at me. "Here. And you better not mess it up. And I noticed you are a little pitchy. If you have any problems, lip sync. Someone who knows what they're doing will sing the part, Princess."

I smirked. She thought she was Randy Jackson or something. When you're as fabulous as I was, you got used to being hated. I would sing with them, and I would show them just how much of a princess I really was. I might not sing in a fancy choir all the time, but I could hold my own. So much for church people being all nice and stuff. It was all good though, because I knew that Jeffrey and I were going to have something special. Jealousy was a terrible thing.

FOURTEEN
Damika

Dana was slipping. She'd told me there were twins, but I didn't remember her saying that they were *foine*. I wasn't really listening, though. My head had been all full of thoughts of Rosheon. They didn't really look all that much alike to me, and James was definitely the geekier and better looking one. I wasn't trying to have no dude all up in my face, but when James kept talking to me, I saw no reason to be rude. He definitely wasn't bad to look at.

After Dana left us standing there, I took a look around the large room. I had no idea how she could find anyone in this room. It was huge and there were so many people in it, I was sure that it was a violation of some building code or a fire hazard. Dana said something over her shoulder and in no time at all, I couldn't see her anymore. She was swallowed up by the crowd. Before I could open my mouth to call out to her, I felt a hand on my arm. It was James. He hadn't moved.

"Don't plan on seeing her again for awhile," he said. I had to look over my shoulder to see who else was near. Was he talking to me?

"Huh?"

"Your friend. Dana. Don't plan on seeing her any time soon. My brother will keep her occupied until church is over. He does that."

"Does what?"

"People are just drawn to him. And he's been talking to Dana, like, all week."

So what was I supposed to do? "I know that she didn't drag me all the way out here to be gone somewhere else the whole time." Anger was bubbling up. I got so mad at Dana sometimes. She could be so self-centered. I was just her excuse to get out of the house, that's all. She knew her mother would probably complain less about her coming here if I was involved, too. She owed me big time.

"You can always hang out with me." I'd almost forgotten that James was still here. Almost, but not quite. Now that I took a closer look at him, the scenery could have been worse.

"Hang out?" I smiled. "Sure, I'll sit with you." That would be better than sitting with a group of total strangers in a church so big. At least I knew his name.

He stepped closer to me. "Did you know that the door over there leads to a courtyard in back of the church?"

I looked over where he was pointing. "So?"

"So we could go sit out there instead of going into the Sanctuary. I do that sometimes. It's not like the Pastor will be saying anything I haven't heard before."

I narrowed my eyes. James obviously thought he had it going on. "I don't know…"

"It'll be fine. The church is big, no one will even notice we're gone."

"And you don't think they'll notice us walk out the door? Just how are we going to do that?"

"This isn't a prison, and people walk in and out all the time." He grabbed my hand. "Just like this."

Part of me didn't want to, but I let myself be led through the thinning crowd and right out the big door at the back of the room. The door slammed shut behind us and with that, it was suddenly quiet. The only sound belonged to a passing car.

"This is much better, isn't it?"

He was right. It was. I hadn't realized how all the commotion in the choir room had stressed me out, even though I'd only been in there a few minutes.

For a building in the middle of Brooklyn, the courtyard was very peaceful. It was like they had gone out of the way to put a tiny little park in the middle of the city. There were even flowers, and several nice benches surrounded by trees. That was a miracle in itself, most of the buildings had just one tree in front of them that had been planted in the middle of cement.

"So now what? We're out. Don't you have to sing or something? Be an usher?"

James shook his head. "That's my brother's thing. He got all of the musical talent in the family. I keep to myself and just sit in the back most of the time. No one will even notice I'm gone."

We sat on a bench near the front of the small courtyard, near the street.

"I know the feeling," I said. "No one misses me either." We were right on the same page, and there was nothing to say at all. Both of us knew what it felt like to be in the shadow of someone popular. The peace was interrupted by my phone vibrating, again. I knew it was Rosheon without looking. "Excuse me." I don't know why, but I was a little embarrassed.

There were three texts, or one long one. I wasn't sure which.

You came all the way out here to sit on some bench with some buster. This doesn't look anything like church to me. Oh, and by the way, you look real nice today. I understand that you don't want to hang out with me, but if that's the case, all you had to do was say so. Who is he anyway?

I gasped, jumped to my feet and looked around for Rosheon.

"What's wrong?" James asked.

My hands trembled. "Nothing," I said. Why was I so afraid? I didn't see Rosheon, but I knew he was somewhere near. Had he followed us all the way to Brooklyn? Even thought it was warm, a chill ran through my body.

"You sure?"

I nodded. I wasn't sure, but he didn't need to know that. "Can we go inside? I'm cold all of a sudden."

"You want my jacket?"

I shook my head. "I just want to go inside."

"Sure. No problem." I looked over my shoulder as we practically ran back toward the building. There was no problem for him, but there certainly might be one for me.

FIFTEEN
Dana

I rocked the solo, that's all there was to it. I was thinking that it was mainly her voice that made Jeffrey be attracted to Michelle, but after what I did, it was all over for her. She might be able to sing, but I had the total package. I really, really liked Jeffrey, and although I had my doubts at first, by the time we left the church Sunday, there was no doubt in my mind that the feeling was mutual.

We went back down to the choir room after church was over. By then I was so hot, I almost wanted to leave without saying anything to Jeffrey. First, he ignored me, and then, he basically threw me into the spotlight. I couldn't tell if he was showing me favor, or just leaving me out there. The other choir members made their feelings obvious. Their hate was so strong I could feel it.

The girl who gave me the robe stared at me. "We'll need your robe back," she said, practically snatching it off my back. I was too through with it all. With Jeffrey's acting all funny and this chick here, I was just ready to go. I was headed to go find Damika when Jeffrey caught me by the door and gave me the widest smile I'd seen in a while. He had the cutest dimple. It was so deep, that I could probably put my tongue in it if I wanted to. And even though I was mad, I sort of wanted to.

"Don't tell me you're tryin' to sneak out without saying goodbye to me. You did great. You didn't tell me you could sing like that. You just said you sounded all right," he said, stepping closer so that I was between him and the wall. I could feel the other girls staring at us from across the room, but I didn't care. They were not happy, and I was sure that Michelle would hear about this soon. I didn't really want to be mad at him anyway, so I played it up. I returned his smile.

"Now, why would I do something like that? I came all this way, of course I would have to say something to you, even though I'm not sure why I should."

"I hope you're not mad about earlier." Jeffrey leaned in and smelled my hair. My heart beat extra fast. "I can't show favoritism among the choir members. At least not during the choir session. I hope you understand that."

"You don't think that what you did was favoritism? You gave me someone else's solo after only hearing me sing a few bars."

"I knew you could handle it. She wasn't coming anyway."

I had to pause and steady myself. His hot breath tickled my ear. I was about to answer him, when Damika and his brother, James walked up.

"Hey, you two," James said. "Don't forget that this is a church. I'd hate to have to throw water on you to separate you."

"Yeah, have some respect," Damika said. She fidgeted a little and seemed really nervous.

I looked from Damika to James. They'd become mighty friendly in such a short time. "Speaking of respect, where have you been? And don't tell me that you were in the sanctuary either. I know you didn't hear us sing, and you sure didn't hear any sermon."

Damika blushed. "You're right," she said. "We were out back sitting on the playground. We were talking and got carried away. Before we knew it, church was over."

James added, "I hope you're not mad at your friend. It's really my fault."

I looked around him, and winked at Damika for confirmation. She'd barely wanted to come and now she was all glued up to some guy she just met. I couldn't blame her though. I could think of worse ways to spend my time.

"Jeffrey," James said. "Can I talk to you for a minute? Do you think you'll be able to tear yourself away for that?"

Jeffrey nodded and they stepped away to whisper to each other. I glared at Damika. "Get any texts lately?" I said jokingly. She didn't laugh.

"I want to leave. I think Rosheon was here." She was shifting all nervously.

I was confused. "What do you mean?"

"I mean, I think he's following me. I think he saw me outside with James, and that's not good."

I frowned. "He doesn't own you."

"This isn't the time or place to discuss this. I want to go home. Can we find your Dad, please?" The sound of her voice scared me. If I didn't know better, I'd think she was about to cry.

Jeffrey and James joined us again, both grinning ear to ear.

"You know, I'm sure my father will be looking for us soon. We need to go meet him."

"We'll walk you." James and Jeffrey spoke at the same time, just like the Double Mint twins.

Damika and I looked at each other and smiled. I felt like I'd woken up in the middle of some Nickelodeon special or something. I looked over my shoulder, and noticed that the girls were staring daggers in my back. I would be doing the same if someone had come out of nowhere and stolen my man.

Jeffrey grabbed my arm and held me back, letting Damika and James go ahead of us. "I really like you," he said.

It was my turn to blush. If he expected me to tell him that I liked him, I wasn't going to do that. I didn't want to seem too eager.

"You think we can hang out?"

"How are we going to do that? You live like two hours away from me on the train." There really was no way for me to get to him from where I lived without taking a bus and several trains. "My mother isn't about to let that happen," I told him.

"I can come get you. I have a car."

Most of my friends were carless. I didn't know how many times my mother had told me that it was just too expensive for me to even consider driving until after I graduated. I'd hit the jackpot with this one. He was fine AND he had a car. "That's what I'm talking about-"

"Well, I share it with my brother," he said, cutting me off. "That's what I was doing, checking with him."

"I don't have a car, so it still sounds good to me, but I don't think my mother is going to let me. She's kind of strict like that."

I could see my mother's face and hear her loud and clear. How many times had she told me not to get in any cars with people? I'd heard the statistics about teen drivers so much that I could probably recite them in my sleep.

He laughed. "I get that. Maybe you can tell her you're going to hang out with your girl. We can go to Starbuck's or something. Tomorrow. After school."

I hesitated. It would be real hard to get Damika to go along with that one. I was tempted though.

"C'mon. It'll be cool. I promise. And I'll get you home before your mother even notices you're late." He smiled again and that big dimple winked at me. "You won't regret it."

How could I resist this fine, caramel-colored hunk that smelled so good? My mother may have warned me about everything under the sun, but she also told me I had to make my own decisions and accept what happened after. "Just coffee, right?"

"You won't regret it. I'll see you tomorrow, around two."

SIXTEEN
Damika

I hope this puppy love of yours is worth it," I told Dana. "You tell me that Rosheon doesn't own me, and you're the one that is lying and cutting school to meet some boy you just met. What's going to happen when your mother finds out? You know what they say, what's done in the dark..." She gave me a 'talk to the hand' palm. "Don't go all church lady on me now."

I shrugged. She just never seemed to think things through. "I just don't like the idea of possibly getting in trouble for something I'm not going to benefit from."

"You'll benefit. I'll owe you. Besides, I have study hall last period, so it doesn't count. It's not exactly cutting, and no one is going to find out unless we tell them."

"Keep telling yourself that," I'd said. That was at lunch, and I hadn't seen her since. I couldn't believe that Damika had put me in this position. She'll owe me for lying for her, again, but I hoped she was enjoying her coffee, if that was really where she and that boy went. She didn't even ask what I was going to do about Rosheon, instead she just left me to lie to my mother about where she was.

I was sweating by the time my mother drove up. "Oh, Dana is staying late at school, Mom. She has to finish her science lab." I tried not to look my mother in the eye because if I did, it would be all over. My mother really could see right through you. It was creepy.

"It's good she's staying on top of things," my mother said.

I headed off her lecture about college. "I've got a lot of stuff to study tonight, too." I knew that would satisfy her. I didn't want to hear one of her rants right now, not with everything that was on my mind. I'd stayed up way too late last night, worrying about Rosheon and ignoring his IM requests. I just didn't want to be bothered with his mess. The fact that he'd followed me was weird and since then, he'd been blowing up my phone so much that I'd just turned both of them off. I'd avoided him all day, but I was going to have to talk to him sooner or later, and I felt pretty sure that time would come as soon as I got home. Otherwise, who knows what crazy mess he'd pull?

I went straight to my room. Hopefully, Dana's mother wouldn't call the house looking for her. I wasn't all that good at lying, so I'd surely be caught if I had to do it again. Since I was already grounded, there was not much left for my mother to do to me except extend my sentence. By the time she was done with me, she would make Rapunzel's imprisonment look like a walk in the park.

I wiggled my mouse to make my computer wake up, and just as I'd thought, there were a dozen missed chats from Rosheon. At least he was consistent, but I couldn't avoid him forever. I closed my bedroom door, then went back to the computer to call him back before he had the chance to call again. I might as well head him off.

The computer rang a few times, then hung up. He didn't answer my chat. I frowned. Really? After all of the times he'd tried to call, you'd think he'd be waiting by his computer. At least I'd tried, but if I knew anything about him at all, I'd hear from him before too long. Just as I settled in to do my homework, the phone Rosheon had given me vibrated, shaking everything on my desktop. I sighed and braced myself before answering.

I could barely get out my hello before Rosheon's voice filled up my ear. "Hey, baby," he said. I was feeling the weirdness from him, but that didn't mean I still didn't feel butterflies on hearing his voice. I didn't want to be, but I was a little excited.

"I just called you on the computer," I said.

"Well, I didn't answer. I'm not there."

"Well, can we talk online later tonight? I don't want my mother to come up here and find me on this phone. She should be home any minute," I lied. She'd driven me home, but he didn't need to know that.

"I was hoping for a few minutes right now."

Of course he was. How bad could a few minutes be? And he didn't sound mad at all anymore.

"You said you're not at home."

"I'm not. Come to your window."

Confused, I took the two steps from my desk to my window. It hadn't been opened in awhile and I had to push so hard I hurt my fingers, but I finally unlocked it and lifted it open. At first what I was seeing didn't register. *What in the world?* I squinted, then realized that I wasn't imagining things. Rosheon was really standing in my back yard. Before I could protest, he climbed up the old cherry tree that covered most of the yard. I stepped back as he swung over and almost jumped through the window into my room.

I put my hand on my chest. If my heart beat any faster, I was sure I'd have a heart attack.

"You can't be in here," I said, my whisper way too loud. "What if my mother comes home? What if a neighbor saw you?" I panicked. "Big mouth Mrs. Miller across the street sees everything."

"Are you avoiding me?" Rosheon stepped toward me and I stepped back, trying not to panic. "Are you afraid? Why? I love you, Damika. I would never hurt you."

I really was home alone. "No, I'm not scared." I wasn't, not really but I was certainly creeped out. I never said he could come into my house, much less through the window. I took a deep breath to try and get it together. *What would Dana do in this situation?* I wondered.

"You have to go. You know you can't be in here. This is real life, not *Twilight* or something. My mother is not going to be understanding about you being up here."

"Not until you answer my question. Are you avoiding me? Are you ashamed of me or something because I haven't been able to talk to you at all? You haven't taken my calls, you haven't been online. Nothing."

"Rosheon, I told you I wasn't." I had to think fast. No matter how mixed my feelings were, my mother was going to kill me. "I've just been really busy with school-"

"And with running off to that church with your buddy, Dana. She's nothing but trouble."

He was making me a little angry now. Who was he to judge my friend? "Well, that may be, but I still have things I'm supposed to be doing. I don't really date anyone, anyway, and definitely not an older guy like you. I just want to get through school."

"Oh, I'm older now? What happened to age not mattering? And you can't tell me you don't enjoy my company."

He was right.

"It's not about that at all," I replied. "I enjoy you and enjoy talking to you. I just don't have a lot of time to do it. My mother is really strict, and as long as I live in her house, I have to do what she says and live by her rules." I couldn't believe I was saying this to Rosheon.

"But your mother liked me." He looked confused for a minute.

"She did, but that doesn't mean she changed her mind about me dating or her rules. I'm trying to be on my best behavior, at least through her birthday." I sighed. "I think I need to take some time and just do what I'm supposed to. This is too stressful for me. You can't be here. And you can't follow me around like you did on Sunday. I feel like you're stalking me."

Rosheon paused, putting his hand on his mouth like he was thinking. "I don't want you to think that. It's just that I thought you liked me, too. I understand if you need some time." He clapped his hands together and rubbed his palms. "Okay then. It's settled. You take whatever you need to get things smoothed out with your mother."

My mouth dropped open. "Really?"

"Yes, really." Rosheon pulled me to him and I stiffened. "I only want the best for you."

I wasn't ready for all this. He kissed me on my forehead and let me go. I forced myself to relax.

"Thank you. I'm glad you get it."

"I get it. And I'm going. I'll wait for you to call me." He took a step back toward the window. "I don't suppose I can go through the door?"

Maybe he didn't get it after all. How in the world would I explain him being in my room or even in the house at all? I wasn't allowed to have normal company without at least giving my family some warning. I shook my head. "Sorry. With my luck you'll run right into my mother, and since she knows what you look like, there is no way you can play that one off."

He nodded. "The window it is, then." Rosheon shimmied his way out of the window and swung back over to the tree. I waited until he was back on the ground to close it.

Maybe I was overreacting, but I somehow didn't think so. I didn't believe for one minute that Rosheon was going away that easily. I watched him slip away from the house and my stomach turned a flip. It certainly was crazy, but part of me was a little excited that he'd gone through all of that trouble just to see me. Had he fallen, he could have been seriously hurt. I was torn, but the Juliette in me was still talking loud and clear. Rosheon had something that was almost too good to resist.

SEVENTEEN
Dana

Starbucks became our spot. Jeffrey didn't seem to do anything after-school but come to see me. I wasn't really sure what love felt like, but this thing with me and Jeffrey had to be close. He was just too hot. I thought about him all day, every day. It was like he'd invaded my brain. Spring was the hardest time of year to pay attention, but since I'd met Jeffrey I was having an even harder time concentrating and couldn't wait for the school day to be over.

"I can't believe you," Damika said during last period. "You're supposed to be such a diva and this dude has got your nose wide open. You act like that chic in those stupid vampire movies."

I narrowed my eyes. She was such a hater. "You're just mad because you're no longer the only one of us having a romance. At least I told you about it. And no one will even raise an eyebrow if they see us together. He's not robbing the cradle and unlike some of us, I don't look like I'm out there dating my daddy."

Her face fell, and I was almost immediately sorry that I'd gone there. Almost, but not quite. She'd been so withdrawn lately, I never knew what was going on with Damika anymore, and I didn't understand why she couldn't support me the way I did her. I'd barely said anything about Rosheon and him pushing her around. She liked him and her mind seemed to be made up. That was good enough for me. So why couldn't Jeffrey be good enough for her? She glared at me, but we didn't talk about it again. Her mother picked her up before I even had a chance to get to the front of the school.

Starbucks was just down the hill from school, and almost every day, Jeffrey was already there when I got there. I wanted to convince The Warden to let Damika go with me, but Damika wasn't having it. She was being on her best behavior, but she still told her mother that I had to go to the library to study. She obviously wasn't that mad at me, but she'd been acting so funny, she might be telling on me any minute. I had no idea what kind of mood she would be in from one day to the next. I had to enjoy things while I could. I could meet with Jeffrey and then make it home before it got dark and before my mother got home. As long as my girl kept up her part of the deal, no one would be the wiser, and so far, so good.

I beat Jeffrey there today. When I got to Starbucks, I searched for him immediately. My heart hit the floor when

I couldn't find him. I hadn't gotten any texts from him cancelling, but my mind still raced. *What if he wasn't coming? What if he'd decided to stand me up?* My conscience screamed at me, but I ignored it. I shook off my doubts and I ordered a tea, then sank into the comfy seats in the corner. I could see practically the whole store from there. *Jeffrey knew better than to try and stand me up*, I told myself. If he didn't already know, someone better tell him that there were a ton of other guys that could take his place.

I must have held my breath for a good ten minutes, but finally, Jeffrey came in. My heart skipped a beat as soon as I spotted him and I went from pouting to smiling inside in two seconds flat. He didn't walk in as much as he blew in; it was as if the whole place turned around to watch him enter. *Damn, he was fine*, I thought. His cap was pulled down to shield his eyes and his hands were down in his pockets. He looked good in his jeans, too. They weren't baggy, but they were still very fashionable. Jeffrey obviously had style. The only thing more appealing than a man with style is one who wore his style like it wasn't planned, and Jeffrey did that well. He looked like looking good was just as natural as could be for him. He wore his swagger like he'd sprayed it on after he stepped out of the shower every day.

"Sorry, I'm late," he said. "Traffic was real bad."

I forced myself not to grin. I didn't want him to think I was too eager, even if I was. "Not a big deal." It wasn't really, but I still had to beat my mother home. I didn't want to seem like a baby, so I kept that to myself. I mean, he *was* driving and I still had a curfew. There weren't that many kids who even had access to a car. It was just too expensive in New York City, or at least that's what my mother had told me, but Jeffrey's parents were obviously from a different planet.

Jeffrey slid into the comfy chair opposite mine, and there was immediately a moment of that awful silence. We had no problem figuring out what to say to each other when we texted or emailed, but in person, I felt suddenly like a goofball, even if we'd been doing this for a minute now. Those first few moments were so weird, but I knew it wouldn't last long.

I suddenly had an idea. "Are you open for something different?" I was ready to take our relationship to the next level, even if I wasn't sure what the next level was. I knew one thing, I was already tired of not being able to be alone with Jeffrey. We saw each other in church or in Starbucks, and in both of those places, there was always a ton of other people around. I was tired of kissing my pillow at night and imagining it was Jeffrey. I was tired of sitting across a wooden table from him with a stupid grin on my face and looking over my shoulder every two seconds. I wanted him to wrap his arms around me and kiss me for real.

A slow smile spread across Jeffrey's face, revealing that too cute, too deep dimple. He ran his tongue across his lower lip before talking and cocked his head to the side. "What did you have in mind?" His voice was so low, it rumbled.

I caught my breath. He had no idea how sexy he was.

My heartbeat drummed loud in my head. "I know somewhere we can go that's more private." I tried to sound as confident as I could. Normally, I was very confident, or I at least acted as if I were, but Jeffrey did things to me that no one else had. He left me feeling not quite balanced, and I loved it. "You're not scared, *are you?*"

He laughed. "I drove forty minutes. I would say that there isn't much I'm afraid of." He paused, and his face changed a little. "I don't want you to get into any trouble, though."

I wanted to pinch myself. I loved that he seemed always to be so concerned about me. It seemed like he was much older than I was, even though we were really only a few months apart. "I'm good," I said. "I can handle my business."

He laughed. "Lead on, Macduff."

I gasped. *That was almost Shakespeare.* My father said that all the time, which kind of creeped me out, but only for a second and just a little. What teenager quoted Shakespeare? I shook it off and we headed back up the hill toward the school.

"Are you sure this is okay?" Jeffrey parked his car across the street from the school steps. He didn't seem so confident once I'd told him all of my plan.

"It's fine. The band is practicing, the theater people are here, too. All of the afterschool stuff is going on so no one will question us at all."

He hesitated. "If you say so, but let the record show that I'm not too sure. You might get slapped on the wrist for being on school property, but I 'm technically trespassing. I don't go here."

"There are almost a three thousand students in this school. No one person can know all of them. What happened to all the Macbeth you were quoting just a few minutes ago?" Was this the same guy who had just thrown me all up in the choir and made me sing without even knowing if I could carry a tune? "It'll be fine. It's not like we're going to be vandalizing the place. We're just looking for a little privacy, right?"

Jeffrey turned off the engine and cracked his windows open just a little. We were parked under a tree, and a slight breeze was blowing. His confidence seemed to be back. Good thing, too, because it was very attractive. I shivered.

"Are you cold?" Jeffrey leaned back in his seat and reached over and rubbed his hands up and down my arms. "We can just stay right here. This is as private as it gets."

I shivered, but this time it was from the chills he was giving me. It wasn't ideal, but he was right. Not many people could even see inside his car, which was probably a good thing. "Well,-"

I never got to finish my thought. Jeffrey had the same idea I did because he leaned over and kissed me so fast, his tongue was in my mouth before I'd even realized what was happening. I almost missed it. I closed my eyes and my head spun. My heartbeat pounded in my ears. I didn't really even have time to start kissing him back.

A loud thud on the car window made us both jump practically out of our skin. We were both shocked back to our corners of the car and I screamed, clutching my chest. I couldn't breathe.

It took a minute for my vision to clear. *What was going on?* That girl from church, the one that Jeffrey supposedly didn't date, Michelle was standing in front of Jeffrey's car, and she looked pissed off. Both of her hands were on the hood and she stood there glaring though the windshield. Her chest was heaving and her hair looked like a bird had done the chicken dance on her crown. If her plan was to grab our attention, she had absolutely succeeded. She hit the car again, this time the hood, with both hands, so hard that I was positive she had to be hurting herself almost as much as she was the car. She had a crazed look on her face and she screamed at the top of her lungs.

"I knew you were no good. I can't believe you would do this to me." She hit the car with each word like she was beating it to death. "Jeffrey, you're no good. And you! I knew you were a ho' the minute I first saw you."

"Jeffrey? What in the world is she talking about?"

He looked as confused as I felt. "She must have followed me. I never told her where I was going."

I wasn't sure whether I should be scared or upset. Why would he have to tell her anything? Michelle seemed to have shed her churchy skin, too. She sounded mad as hell. "Did you tell anyone?" I asked.

He nodded. "My brother. I had to tell him something."

"I thought you said that she wasn't your girlfriend?" From the looks of things, she was mad as hell. If she wasn't his girlfriend, I couldn't think of anything that would make her as mad as she looked.

Michelle paced in front of the car. "Come out here and look me in my eye."

Jeffrey was frozen. All of the color left his face. He wore a look of disbelief, almost like he couldn't make sense of what was happening at all.

"Are you going to do something?" I asked finally.

He jumped, as if my words were a slap across his face that brought him back to his senses.

"She'd better stop or she's going to dent my car."

Michelle had moved around to Jeffrey's window by now and she was slapping on it with her open palms. I was suddenly angry. This crazed girl was calling me every name in the book and all he could think about was his stupid car?

"You obviously have some business to handle, so I'm going to let you do that. Her? She needs to get her life and leave mine the hell alone."

I didn't need any of this, and there was no way I was going to make a scene over some boy. I could hear my mother now, not to mention that we were in front of my school. There was no telling who was still around. This might be all over the place by tomorrow.

I opened the door to get out and as soon as I opened the door, Michelle ran around the car in my direction.

"Wait!" Jeffrey tried to stop me. He grabbed at the end of my sweater, but missed. Michelle ran right up to me. I closed the door behind me and practically fell right into her. She was so close that I could smell her anger. I backed up so far I was wedged between her and the car.

"Dana, is that your name?" she yelled. "You need to keep your scrawny butt away from my man."

My face heated up. Who in the hell was she calling scrawny? And he was her man, now? Clearly one of them was lying to me.

Jeffrey moved so fast that I never saw him move. He pulled her backward, away from me. Michelle fought him like a crazy person. Her arms and legs were going every which way so fast that I was confused. I couldn't tell if Jeffrey was fighting back or defending himself from Michelle. She'd obviously totally lost her mind.

My face burned with embarrassment. I'd somehow been thrown into the middle of a bad episode of a Jerry Springer show. Things had gone from wonderful to unbelievable in the blink of an eye. As badly as I'd wanted to see Jeffrey, I now wanted to get away from him as fast I could. This kind of drama was just not hot. I loved to be the center of attention, but attention and drama were not the same thing, and what was going on here was nothing but messy. Not my thing at all. There was no way I could be seen fighting out in the street, and certainly not over a guy.

Michelle fell and landed on her butt, skidding backward on the sidewalk. She started to yell. "I know you didn't just throw me on the ground!"

Jeffrey stepped toward her, trying to calm her down.

I knew an opening when I saw it. My heartbeat pounded in my ears so loudly that I couldn't hear anything else. I'd never been one to let a good thing get away and I wasn't going to start now. While they were busy dealing with whatever it was that was going on between them, I walked away.

I didn't turn back, look over my shoulder, pass go or collect two hundred dollars. Michelle falling on her butt was my Get-Out-of-Jail-Free card. Right now, her problem was with Jeffrey, and that was where it needed to stay. She was crazed and there was no telling what she might do if she had time to think about it.

Jeffrey was *fine*, but I knew better. I practically ran up the block and crossed the street just as I got to the corner. My heartbeat slowed down. I couldn't hear Michelle's shrieks anymore. As I slipped around the corner, I finally looked back. Michelle was standing up now, but from the way her arms were flailing around in the air, it was obvious she was still upset.

Part of me felt bad for Jeffrey. That girl was so clearly not stable. I didn't have time to even contemplate that Jeffry had lied to me. I could deal with that later. It didn't matter what his words said. I wasn't sure if he'd lied to me, but Michelle's actions were speaking loud and clear. He might think he wasn't dating her, but in her mind, she was obviously still dating him.

EIGHTEEN
Damika

I could hear my mother's laughter all the way upstairs in my room. She was so serious sometimes that I thought I was mistaken at first. I sat very still and listened hard for a few minutes.

There it was again.

My mother, The Warden, was laughing. I was upstairs in my room trying to do my homework and stay out of trouble, and my peace was being punctuated by this alien sound in my house. My mother was downstairs, and as far as I knew, she was alone. There was no television on and I don't think she'd been drinking, but there was no doubt that the unfamiliar sound that I was hearing was laughter from the even more unlikely place that was my parental unit.

I'd read it was possible for some mothers to just have a breakdown. What if that was happening to her? I stood up slowly, then moved as quickly as I could to the landing at the top of the stairs. I didn't want to eavesdrop, but I needed to know what was so funny that it had my mother acting so totally not like herself. I stood there and listened so hard I could hear the house creak around me. Finally, I couldn't stand it anymore. I called down to her. "Mom? Did you call me?" I asked.

She didn't answer. I frowned. I couldn't hear anyone down there with her, but I could clearly hear the hum of her voice, and she sounded happier than usual for a weeknight. Since dad died, she didn't have a whole lot of phone-type friends. Most of her friendships happened at church. I took a deep breath and made my way downstairs.

She was in the kitchen, sitting at the table, the phone pressed to her hear. Her back was to the door, but she laughed when I entered, so engrossed in her conversation that she didn't even hear me come in. "You can stop trying to flatter me," she said, then laughed again. "You know you young men…"

I cleared my throat to let her know that I was there. I really didn't want to hear what I thought I was hearing. If my mother was talking to some guy other than her dead like this, I certainly didn't want to know it. She was a woman of God. She told me this all the time. And I wasn't ready for her to date. She was an upstanding citizen. My mother did the right thing. Always. That's what mothers did.

My racing thoughts were interrupted before she got a chance to turn around. "Rosheon–'

I almost passed out. "What?" This was starting to really creep me out.

She spun around then. "Oh. Damika just walked in. Hey baby."

I forced myself to be calm. "Are you talking to Rosheon, Mom?" There had to be some explanation why my mother was obviously flirting on the phone with my boyfriend. Why was he even calling my house? Or had she called him? That was an even more frightening thought.

"I am," she said. "He called to wish me a happy birthday."

"But it's not your birthday."

"I know that. Isn't that funny?"

I was confused. I hadn't spoken to Rosheon in a minute, especially after that room thing, so why in the world was my mother chatting with him like he was her best friend? He'd just called to get at me, I was sure of it, so why was I suddenly so jealous? I took a deep breath and tried to get a handle on all of the conflict I was feeling inside. He couldn't possibly really be chatting up my mother, and she couldn't be seriously letting him. She was *old. So is he*, the voice in my head said

I'd ignored all his calls and texts on my phone and had completely turned off the phone that he'd given me. I got it. This was an attempt to get my attention. I was practically seeing red; it had worked.

"Mom, I think I'm going to go to the library. I promised Dana that I'd meet her there to study for our bio test. Is that okay?" I spoke extra loud. I wanted Rosheon to hear me.

She waved me away. "Take your phone. And be back by eight. It's a school night." She turned her back to me and went back to her conversation like I'd barely even been there and the whole thing was an ordinary occurrence.

I tried to contain my fuming. I left my mother in the kitchen and ran upstairs to grab by phone and my jacket. By the time I left the house, she was still on the phone, but if I knew Rosheon, he'd meet me at the library. He'd certainly gone through a lot to get my attention, and he was successful. He was crazier than I'd imagined, but I don't think he was counting on *my* special kind of crazy. What did he think this was? He had no right to be calling my mother. And I didn't even want to begin to talk about her. She wasn't supposed to be laughing and joking with Rosheon. She was supposed to protect me from him and give him a piece of her mind for even daring to call our house. And what'd happened to my punishment? After days and days of watching over my every breath, it was suddenly okay for me to go to the library by myself, without her driving me? Not that I was complaining.

I practically ran the three blocks to the library and burst into the small building way too loudly. There weren't too many people there, about five or six, but half of those looked up and glared at me as I were committing some kind of sin just by disturbing their space. I don't know what I expected, but I didn't find it. I circled the room twice, but Rosheon wasn't there. My anger changed to disappointment. I fought back the sting in my nose that could too easily have turned to tears.

I was just about to plop down into a chair to sulk when Rosheon walked in. Anger mixed with a feeling a relief that he'd showed. Confused, I pursed my lips. I was supposed to be angry, not happy to see him. Names for Rosheon that were everything but his name swam through my mind. I wanted to call him everything under the sun, but the wide smile of his lush lips wouldn't let me. Instead, I stood my ground and watched him make his way over to me. The way he walked still looked good to me, even though I really wanted to punch him in the face.

I crossed my arms across my chest before he started talking. "You've been avoiding me," he said.

"What did you think I'd do, Rosheon? You've been scary. First you followed me to church, then you crawl though my window..."

The librarian glared at us from behind the desk as she made a loud shushing sound.

"And now my mother.' I gripped the back of the chair I held onto so tightly that all color was leaving my hands. I couldn't even find words to say how I felt. "You can't be serious." I couldn't tell if I was mad at him, or just hurt. It felt like he'd been cheating on me with my best friend. Scratch that. A best friend would have been less hurtful than my mother.

"We were just talking." His eyes pleaded with me. "It's the only way I knew of to get close to you."

The librarian shushed us again. I knew I shouldn't be buying what he was saying, but that sorry smile of his was already knocking down the wall I'd built between us.

"Can we go outside?" Rosheon lowered his voice. "I promise I won't do anything crazy."

I grabbed my phone off the table where I'd placed it, juggled it with my books and my bag, and we trudged outside, a lot more quietly than I'd come in. Inside, I was all confused. Outside, I fumed, but a big part of me was still happy to see Rosheon, and that complicated things. Everything about him told me that I should walk away, but my head and my heart didn't seem to be listening to one another at this moment.

He held the door for me and I tripped across the threshold, almost dropping everything, outside. Rosheon stepped forward and grabbed the stack in my hand. "Let me take this for you," he said.

I hoped he didn't think a little chivalry would get him out of the doghouse. I held onto my few things like I was holding onto my life. Rosheon and I locked eyes, and I relaxed my grip. I kept my eyes focused on him and we didn't say anything as I slowly followed him to his car. He was like the Pied Piper, but the only music was inside my head.

I had to make Rosheon understand that I wasn't happy with how he'd been acting. None of this was okay. It wasn't okay for him to follow me, show up unexpectedly, talk to my mother on the phone or ignore me when I said I couldn't or didn't want to see him. It was clear to me, but didn't seem to be so clear to him at all.

We stood for a minute without talking. "Can you go for a drive?"

I hesitated. "Rosheon, I have to get home."

"I promise, all I want to do is talk. Your mother thinks you're at the library. I'll bring you back here in an hour. Please. I can't imagine being without you."

My heart skipped a beat. He sounded so real. "One hour?"

He nodded, then smiled.

I hesitated. Every part of my body screamed that I should just walk away. "You know…"

I couldn't' finish my sentence. Rosheon grabbed me by the arm and all of the alarms in my head started ringing. "I said I'm not going to hurt you. I just want to talk."

I pulled back from him, practically seeing red. He dropped all my books and everything else he was carrying. Who did he think he was?

"You are hurting me now. Stop it." My mind raced. There was no way I was going to let anyone handle me the way he was doing. "Let me go, Rosheon."

He didn't answer. Instead, in almost one movement, Rosheon yanked his car door open and practically threw me inside so hard, I almost landed clear across in the driver's seat. Pain shot through my side as I slammed into the console in the middle. By the time I sat up, Rosheon had slammed the door and made it almost around to the driver's side of the car.

My head swam. He yanked his door open, slid inside and started the car, pulling away from the curb so fast that he had to be breaking some law.

I rubbed my arm. "What the hell, Rosheon? You couldn't have asked nicely?"

"I'm so sorry," he said. "I got a little carried away. I didn't think you would listen to me."

I hit him in the back of the head, and he cringed. "Next time, you ask me, or we are going to have some problems. All you had to do was ask."

He slowed down and pulled over. Rosheon had both hands on the steering wheel as he stared out the front window without looking at me.

"I hope you'll forgive me. It's just that you're so beautiful, and I can't imagine losing you." His voice softened and I could swear that he was holding back a sob. "I just want you to listen to what I have to say, and if you don't like it, I promise I'll leave you alone for good. Deal?"

The car was silent as I contemplated his words. My arm and side both hurt, but in that moment, I felt more loved than I ever had, and somehow very powerful. It probably wasn't the best thing to do, but what could it hurt to listen, right? I nodded. I could handle Rosheon. I'd just have to deal with my mother later.

NINETEEN
Dana

I had to talk to Damika. She would know what to do in situations like this. She was the most levelheaded person I knew. I walked home slowly, alternating between looking over my shoulder and dialing Damika's number. I don't know what I was expecting. Jeffrey was probably too embarrassed to follow me, but I couldn't say that for Michelle. Who knows, as crazy as she seemed to be, she might kick his behind and then try to start on mine.

Just to be sure, I went home a way I normally didn't. I certainly didn't need her and Jeffrey rolling up to my house bringing all that drama with them. My mother would lose her mind.

Damika never answered her phone. I tried four times and got more annoyed at every ring. I was always there for her, so where was she when I needed her? I knew I was being unreasonable. Her phone was probably dead or something, anyway.

My house was quiet. I dropped my bag by the front door and then I tiptoed in, trying to get up to my room. I wanted some time to process things, and I was generally tired. All of this drama was new to me. Every now and then, someone would get on my nerves or we might have a little disagreement, but I'd never been involved in any of this Jeffrey-Michelle Jerry Springer type mess. Out in the street, at that. You never can tell about a person. I thought I knew Jeffrey, but what kind of person was he if he was involved with someone who made the kinds of scenes that Michelle had? I mean, we were teenagers, not middle-aged people fighting over husbands and wives. And who did that anyway, outside of television and *Love and Hip Hop*?

My head was down when reached my room, so I didn't notice both my mother and Dennis sitting on my bed. Dennis cleared his throat and I stopped in my tracks. My mouth dropped open. They never came into my room. Maybe my mom, but certainly not him.

"What's going on?" I swallowed hard. "Is somebody dead?"

My mother jumped to her feet. I knew the look on her face. She was pissed. Instinctively, I glanced over my shoulder to make sure that nothing stood between me and the door, in case I needed to escape, and I stopped breathing mid-breath. My father was standing outside my door. I'd been so preoccupied, I didn't even know that he was in the house or notice his car outside.

"You can't run from me, Dana, so don't even try it." My mother paused, then took a step closer. The silence in the room magnified and the only thing I could hear was my own breath inside my head. "Do you want to start talking?"

"Huh?"

"You have to do better than that."

My eyes widened. What had I done that my mother could possibly know about? I was at a loss. I'd been in class when I was supposed to, done all of my crazy chores and hadn't failed anything that I knew of.

"I'm confused Mom." I looked at my father for help, but he was stone-faced. My mother was sort of crazy anyway, but when she was angry, she might as well be possessed with her head spinning around on her shoulders.

"I'm disappointed in you, Dana. I thought we had an understanding. A talk. I expect more from you than-"

I shook my head and cut her off. "Than what? I didn't do anything, I promise."

Dennis stood up. "Don't interrupt your mother."

I had to grip my dresser to try and not lose it. Who was he anyway? He didn't know anything about me.

She narrowed her eyes. I hated it when we played guessing games.

"Would you just tell me what you think I did?" My mother moved and I flinched. It wasn't beyond her to slap me.

"Well, Dennis met up with our nosey neighbor across the street on his way in this evening and do you know what she had the privilege of witnessing today?"

A sense of dread settled on me. How could she possibly know anything? I shook my head and my eyes welled up with tears.

She continued. "I get home, expecting to be able to relax, and find out that my daughter who is supposed to be staying after school to study is fighting in the street like a common trollop!"

There it was. I knew she was beyond pissed off when she started speaking like she was from the Dark Ages. The room closed around me and my mother suddenly was bigger than life. My mind raced.

"I-I'-"

"Close. Your. Mouth." She slapped the dresser with her fist as she talked, each pound echoed through my body as if she'd hit me directly. I cringed. "How embarrassing is it for me to find out that my daughter was outside in a public place acting like a Ghetto Queen? What must people think of me?"

My father finally spoke. "Give the girl a chance," he said. "I'm sure she has a good explanation for this."

My face stung as I fought to keep back my tears. I know I was wrong to lie about hanging out with Jeffrey, but where was the concern for *me*? Anything could have happened to me out there and all she cared about was how I made *her* look?

She wasn't done. "We are going to be the laughing stock of the block."

I couldn't take it anymore. "What about me, Mom? You don't even seem to care what I do as long as I don't get caught doing it. What about how I feel?" Tears streamed down my face now. "It wasn't exactly pleasant for me to have some maniac come yelling at me and trying to kill me."

Both she and Dennis stood up suddenly. "Are you raising your voice to me?"

I recoiled. If it were possible, steam would be coming from her ears. Dennis had a crazed look in his eyes, like he wasn't sure what he'd gotten himself into.

I glanced over my shoulder, toward the door. I could run, but there was nowhere for me to go, really, so that idea disappeared as quickly as it had come. Dennis put his hand on my mother's shoulder, and that seemed to calm her some.

"We are concerned about you, baby," my father said, finally stepping in. "There are lots or problems with this whole situation. First, you never told us you were going to Starbuck's. If something happened, we would have no idea where to even begin looking-"

"That and you lied. You cut class, and you were acting like a thug." My mother was getting louder again.

"Mom, I wasn't. She stepped to me." I fought to hold back the tears that were filling up my eyes. Nothing I said was going to make her understand.

"You're grounded," my mother said. "I can't deal with this now. I'll figure out the rest later." She stuck out her hand, palm up and waited.

She didn't have to say the words. I knew what that meant. I took my phone out of my back pocket and gently laid it in her palm, my stomach twisting as I handed it over. Grounded was no big deal. I was always home, but taking my phone, well, she might as well just cut off my air.

"Mom, everyone has phones. How am I supposed to communicate with my friends?"

"I don't care. Smoke signal." My mother stormed away and Dennis followed her like she was his duck-mother and he'd imprinted on her. I stood my ground, not sure what to do next. Waiting to find out my fate was the worst. My mother hadn't reacted to anything with such emotion in a long while, and I was certainly more afraid of her than I was Michelle.

As I sat on the edge of my bed, tears flowed silently down my face. I was wrong, but I wanted my mother to have my back. I wanted to be able to talk to her like those girls on television talked to their parents when things went wrong, but I knew she would never hear what I had to say now.

My father hadn't left with them. Instead, he came quietly into my room and sat on the edge of the bed. He cleared his throat.

"So was she much bigger than you. Did she win the fight?"

The tears still flowed, but I laughed just a little. He always did know the right thing to say. "She was basic, too, Dad. You should have seen her."

A look of confusion crossed over his face. "Basic?"

I flopped on the bed next to him. "Yes, just not but together or anything."

"Snaggletooth?" He rubbed his hand across my back, and I laughed again.

"Thanks, Dad."

"No problem, Dana. Let me guess, was all of this over a guy?"

I paused and looked up at him. Dad had a way of being the level-headed one when things were mad crazy. I missed him. "You really want to hear it? You'll probably think its silly."

He looked me in the eye. "Dana, you are the most important person in the world to me. Of course I want to hear it. And if it's important to you, it's important to me."

I licked my lips and took a deep inhale and told him everything. About the choir, Jeffrey and his brother. Cutting class. And Michelle.

My father listened without so much as a grunt. He didn't comment and he didn't judge, Instead, he waited patiently for me to finish and then he said. "You done?"

I nodded.

"You really liked him, huh?"

"I did, Dad. But I don't think I can trust him. And now I can't even go back to that church with you-"

"No, Ma'am, that's not true. I don't want you to ever let some triflin' people like these keep you from doing something you want to do. I have to admit I'm a little crushed that you weren't coming to the church for me."

I laughed again. I felt better already. "Sorry, Dad."

"Does your mother know?"

I shook my head.

He paused. "Okay, you know what I would do if I were you? I'd put on my best outfit and stride right on up into that church, say hello to both of those kids like nothing happened, give them a huge smile and then keep on going. Take the high road, and don't let that girl think she scared you away."

I frowned. "I'm not so sure."

He stood up. "I am. But that Jeffrey, he's got some growing up to do. He should have stood up to that girl. He's not worth it if he can't stand up and say what he wants, Dana. And if his choice isn't you, you have to respect that." He paused. "I have to go Dana, but promise me one thing?"

"What, Dad?"

"No more cutting class." His mouth formed into a hard, thin line.

"Okay."

"So, I'll see you Sunday? I'm guessing you will be singing Michelle's solo."

I shrugged. "I have no idea. What about Wanda? Is she going to?"

He shook his head. "Not with me. We broke up. I'm taking the high road, too. We'll both be some finely dressed polite people, but if you're singing, I can invite you mother and, um…"

I smiled. "Dennis, Dad."

"Yeah, him." He winked, slipping his arm around my shoulders.

"The high road?"

My dad kissed me on the forehead, like he used to do when I was small. "The high road, baby girl."

TWENTY
Damika

The "American Idol" music played on the television and I pushed my panic button. I was in trouble for sure. I jumped to my feet.

"Rosheon," I shouted, "How could you let it get this late?"

"Relax. We'll figure it out." He barely seemed concerned at all.

He'd obviously returned back to the crazy man that had tossed me in the car earlier. Rosheon had no idea what my mother was capable of. I searched through the pillows on the hotel room couch, tossing them on the floor. "Where's my phone? Oh, God! You said an hour." We were obviously well past that. "I am so dead."

He had no idea. There *was* no we. When it came time to face the music, I would be the one standing in front of The Warden, preparing to do my penance alone. I lifted up his cushions, searching for where my phone had gone, and then it dawned on me. Rosheon had been holding it when he dropped my books. I gasped. My phone was somewhere out there in the world, outside that library. There was no telling who had it by now. There was also no way of me knowing how many times my mother had called or texted me on it.

"I need to call my mother." I tried not to panic. "No, I need to text Dana. That will be the first place my mother calls if she hasn't already. Dana needs to know what's up."

Rosheon reached over to the desk by the side of the sofa, handing me his phone. "Use mine."

I reached for it and winced. My side ached. I was going to be sore tomorrow. A few beads of sweat popped onto my forehead. I was sure that I was going to be grounded until I was forty for this.

I paced the room as I dialed, then listened to Dana's voice mail. There was no telling what she was doing, but I hung up without leaving a message and then dialed her back. No answer again. Where was she? She had to be home from hanging out with Jeffrey by now. Maybe she was angry because I'd given her a hard time about her "puppy love" romance, but if I called her more than once, she would know it was an emergency and take my call. We had disagreements all the time, but she was still my girl. I was sure of it. She owed me more than a few anyway since I'd been covering for her all the time since she'd met Jeffrey. Her mother probably still thought she was with me afterschool or at the library.

Rosheon hovered not far away. "Maybe she doesn't recognize the number and won't answer that."

That made sense to me. I quickly sent her a text.

It's Damika. If my mother asks, I'm with you.

I handed him back his phone. "I need to go home. Can you drop me back near my house?" My mind was working fast. What kind of spin could I put on this to make it okay with my mother?

Rosheon pulled me to him. I wasn't angry at him anymore. That had passed at least an hour ago and now I had other things to worry about. After the first thirty minutes, he'd worked his magic and I could no longer remember why I was mad at him, anyway. I mean, he just wanted to see me. He made me feel special and I liked being with him. Every relationship had its ups and downs, so we just had to work through ours. I inhaled and enjoyed his smell as we hugged. He ran his hands up and down my back, sending shivers all through me.

"Can I ask you a question?"

"That *was* one." I half-smiled. "But I gotta go soon."

"Will you be in more trouble if you are later, rather than leaving now? Or will the amount of trouble be the same? I'm not ready for you to go yet, and I don't think you're ready to face your mother. Why don't we stay here and work on it awhile?"

I'd already resolved that I was in major trouble, a new kind that I hadn't experienced before. As far as my mother was concerned, I'd probably just disappeared. If I didn't tell her where I was, I'd be in trouble. If I did tell her where I was, I'd *still* be in trouble. It couldn't get any worse. Rosheon kissed my neck and I shivered. "Just a few minutes more, then we gotta go, okay?"

He didn't answer, instead he trailed kisses down my neck, and I felt like the most beautiful girl in the city, instead of the too smart, sometimes awkward sidekick with bad skin that I'd seen in the mirror earlier.

TWENTY
Dana

Someone was banging on the front door. It was so loud that I could hear it all the way up in my bedroom. I'd stayed there after my disagreement with my mother. It wasn't like I was hiding; I did have homework to get done, but I waiting for her to tell me what my punishment was. If she said I was going to be punished, I believed her. This was too big to just go away. I could have done a lot of things, but embarrassing my mother in public was high on her list of transgressions. Resisting it would be worthless.

She'd taken my phone, and I didn't dare go online. I was basically an electronic prison, cut off from the matrix and all my friends. I didn't' know if Jeffrey had tried to contact me or not, and I had no way of talking to Damika. Not that she would want to talk to me. I hadn't exactly been nice to her after her crazy remarks about my relationship with Jeffrey. She acted like she knew so much. She'd never even had a boyfriend before Rosheon started coming around, so I don't know how she thought it as okay to tell me what to do.

The knocking was replaced by hushed voices. I frowned. We never had visitors at this time of night. I tried to ignore the noise and turned back to my history book. Whatever was going on really wasn't my problem, and both of the parental units were downstairs anyway. They could answer the door. I had bigger things to worry about. I mean, if Michelle had followed Jeffrey, what if she knew where I lived? Just how crazy was she? Let her try and get through my mother.

"Dana!" My mother shrieked from the bottom of the stairs, her voice all nasally and mean. I cringed. She would never think to actually come up the stairs to tell me what she had to say. "Could you come down here?"

I dragged myself from across the bed where I'd been studying and headed downstairs, not really sure what I was being summoned for. My mother was standing just inside the door, and Damika's mother was sitting in the chair we kept in the front hallway. She was bent over, her head in her hands. My mother stood close with her hand on the woman's back. I slowed down. Nothing about the situation looked like it was good.

She raised her head just as I reached the bottom step. Damika's mother's face was streaked with tears.

My own mother had that business face on. "When's the last time you talked to Damika?"

I shook my head. "What's going on?"

"We don't know where Damika is." Her mother's voice quivered. "She went out to the library earlier and never came home."

I frowned. "Just call her." Not coming home on time is something that I would do, not Damika. She usually followed at least most of the rules.

I shrugged. I couldn't remember what I was supposed to say. Damika hadn't told me anything. "Have you called her? She usually answers her phone."

Damika's mother slowly raised her hand. She was holding her daughter's phone. I gasped.

"The librarian called me from it and I went to get it. She apparently dropped it outside the library."

"She went to the library? But it's been closed for hours," I said. Neither one of us were generally separated from our phones too long, unless our parents took them from us as a punishment. Things started to move in slow motion. If Damika was away from her phone, I could only imagine what was going on, but I didn't want to get her in any more trouble.

My mother looked at me so hard it felt as if she were looking through me. "Weren't you with her after school, Dana? The two of you were supposed to be studying together, right?"

Damika's mother spoke up. "No, I drive Damika home after school. I have been for awhile now. She was being punished. I drove Dana a few times, too, but the last few times, Damika said Dana had to stay after school to study."

I took a step back. The lies were closing in around me.

"Really?" my mother said. "'She told me that she was studying with Damika. Isn't that right, Dana?"

I choked on my words. "Well, not exactly."

"What does not exactly mean, Dana? Either you were with Damika, or you weren't. Either you were studying, or you weren't. Which is it?"

I hung my head in shame. There was no way I could talk or tap dance my way out of this. "Neither one."

My mother glared at me. I was digging my hole deeper and deeper. "Do you know where Dana is?" She spoke loudly, as if I was hard of hearing and she had to make it simple for me. "If there is something going on and you know about it, you'd better tell us. Was she with you when you had your little altercation in the middle of the street? The librarian said that Damika got into the car with some guy."

I gasped again. They stared me down. My mother's face was as hard as a rock, and Damika's mother looked stricken. "A guy?"

"Are you hard of hearing now, Dana? Yes. A man. The librarian told the police that it looked like they might have been arguing. She had to shush them a couple of times before they finally went outside." My mother slowed down again. "Do you know who that could have been? None of your friends have cars as far as I know."

I had a bad feeling in the pit of my stomach. If I did tell them, my mother might send me to a convent and Damika might be pissed at me. I knew she'd gone with Rosheon. Where else could she be? We knew just about everything about each other, and frankly, there was not that much excitement in her life lately. I could be wrong, since she hadn't told me about Rosheon really until she was forced to, but I doubt it.

On the other hand if I did tell them what I thought, my mother might send me to a convent anyway. Damika could be in danger. When I saw Rosheon, he'd just been a little too rough for my tastes. Damika had actually had a bruise on her arm the next day. He'd also followed us to church in Brooklyn and who knows what else. Normally, we wouldn't give each other up that easily, but sometimes, I had to go with my gut feeling.

"I think she's with that guy, Rosheon. The one she met online."

Both women gasped. Damika's mother's hand flew up to her mouth. "I was just talking to him," she said. "She met him online? They didn't tell me that?" She looked as if she might faint.

It was my turn to be surprised. "Really? I would think you wouldn't want him around us. I mean, he's old. She didn't tell me either, not until he showed up after school."

"Well, nineteen is older than I'd wish for my daughter, but I wouldn't call him old, exactly."

I paused. Damika did say that she was surprised that her mother had been so friendly toward Rosheon. "I thought he was much older than that."

"Dana, what are you talking about? If you knew that she was hanging out with this Rosheon person, why didn't you say anything? What would people think?"

I swallowed hard, opening and closing my fist. There it was again, my mother's main concern. She was more worried about what other people thought than she was about what was going on with me and my friends. I was so mad, I had to fight back tears. My mother kept talking at me, but her words blurred together. I felt as if I was watching us from outside my body. Finally, I couldn't take it.

"Why would I tell you anything, Mom? You never hear me. All you care about is yourself and what the neighbors think! If I'd told you that I saw Rosheon pushing her around, what would you have done? Huh? Ground me? Home-school me? Tell me I couldn't be around her anymore? You wouldn't have done a damn thing!"

My mother's palm connecting with my face stopped my tirade in mid-shriek and brought me back to myself. I fell backward and just missed hitting my head on the bottom of the staircase.

Damika's mom jumped to her feet. "That's enough." She rushed over to me. "This isn't solving anything, Deneen. Just stop it." Tears rolled down her face.

Dennis came from wherever he'd been. "What's going on?" He stopped between the two women and looked down at Mrs. Woods as she cradled my head in her hands.

"Just stop it. We have to find Damika. I have a bad feeling. Dana," she sobbed in between words. "Please. Tell me. Help me."

There was no sound, only Mrs. Woods' sobs. My mother stood behind us, watching, a blank look on her face. Dennis was the one to break the awful silence.

"Dana?"

I nodded, got up from the floor and sat next to Damika's mother on the steps. I started at the beginning. Again.

TWENTY ONE
Damika

Rosheon had three more minutes or I was going to find a way to take a bus home. I was beginning to feel like he had no intention of taking me anywhere. Every ten minutes or so, we were back where we started, and his kisses were starting not to feel that good anymore. As it stood, I had all of my clothes on, and he was shirtless. His pants were still on, but his belt was undone and his pants were hanging open. It was well past midnight and I was sure there was no excuse on earth that my mother would buy now.

"I can wait until you're ready," he said. "But can you do me this one favor? You can't leave me hanging like this. Oral is not sex."

If he thought I was going to put my mouth anywhere below his waist, he was out of his mind. That was just disgusting. "Um, no, Rosheon. I don't think that's for me. I'm not the one. And besides, in my mind, any time a part of you is inside a part of me, that's sex. I don't know you like that."

"You don't know me now?" Rosheon folded his arms across his chest and pouted like a baby, then went into the small bathroom and closed the door behind him. I got up from the desk chair and walked to the window. The hotel room overlooked the runway at JFK Airport. When we'd first come in, it was romantic, now it was just annoying. The illumination from the runway and surrounding lights was beautiful, but the night behind it was a reminder of how far past library closing hours we really were. I ran my finger up the bridge of my nose and paused it at that spot between my eyes, pressing my fingers into it. My head was pounding. I knew it didn't compare to the pounding my mother was going to give me. I was going to be punished until I was forty.

I listened to the thud in my head so intently that it took me a minute to realize that I was really hearing real pounding. Someone was at the door.

"Rosheon? Are you expecting someone?"

He didn't answer.

This was getting worse by the minute. I couldn't believe that I'd gotten into his car in the first place. The pounding became more insistent.

"One minute, please." I straightened my clothes, then snatched the door open, prepared to curse out a hotel employee. Two uniformed policeman stopped the words in my throat.

"We're looking for Rosheon Davison. Can we come in?"

I had no idea what to say. If it were possible for all of the color to drain from my face, I'm sure it would have. All I could do was nod as a feeling of dread took over my body.

Rosheon stepped from the bathroom at that point. His head was down, but he looked up and was immediately paralyzed.

The policeman walked around me. "Rosheon Davison?" they asked.

Rosheon nodded slowly.

"You are under arrest. Back up slowly and put your hands on the wall."

"I don't understand," I said.

Rosheon moved backed slowly. "I didn't do nothing."

"Who is Angelo Greenfield?" The larger office put his hand on his gun holster.

"My brother-in-law?"

"Well, you checked in under that name and used a credit card in that name to pay for the room."

"I can explain."

"They always can," the officer said. "Are you going to be difficult? We wouldn't want the young lady here to see you beat up for resisting arrest. And you must be Damika Woods right?"

I almost peed my pants. "I haven't done anything. I need to get home."

"We know. We used the text messages you sent to your friend to track you guys down. You mother is very worried. Just have a seat for a minute." He turned back to Rosheon just as his partner was slapping the handcuffs on his wrist and took a small card from his pocket. "Rosheon Davison, you are under arrest for credit card fraud, theft of services, assault, predatory behavior and indecency with a minor. You have the right to remain silent. Anything you say can and will be used against you in a court of law."

"I didn't do anything. You have no proof. Damika, I'm sorry. Don't believe them."

"This time, I think we do have proof."

"What do you mean?" Rosheon stammered. "There's nothing."

The cop interrupted. "Maybe not on your end, but your little friend here has a computer registry and cell phone logs full of all sorts of things that could be considered evidence. You might have erased yours, but once it's out there, it never goes away. You, Mr. Catfisher, have been caught in your own net."

This time? Tears started flowing down my face. I guess I wasn't as special as I'd thought. I felt so naked standing there. Clearly they had gone through my phone already, and maybe my computer, too. The pictures I sent Rosheon over the last few weeks flashed in my head. They weren't bad, not exactly, but they weren't good either. If they found them on my computer, where else had they found them? How was I going to explain this to my mother? I was dead.

The officer continued reading Rosheon his rights.

Between the pounding in my head and the sounds of my crying, I couldn't hear anything else.

DISCUSSION QUESTIONS

1. How do you think Rosheon knew where Damika lived, and should she have been alarmed the first time he showed up at her house, uninvited?

2. Many cell phones use location tracking devices when you post to social media, so it's not unusual for someone with bad intentions to be able to tell where you are by what you post and what you say. What are some ways you can avoid this?

3. A Catfish is someone who uses an online personality and picture that is not their own. It is not uncommon for a people to use very attractive pictures as a substitute for their own. What would you have done when Rosheon wasn't who he said he was?

4. At the end of the story, the arresting officer told Rosheon "Once it's out there, it's out there," in reference to his texts and other messages to Damika. It is true that things you do online and in text stick around forever? What are some ways you can avoid having what you do now as a young person from affecting you when you older?

5. What are some examples of things it's not okay to post online or text and how could these things posses a problem for you later?

6. Damika sent questionable pictures of herself to Rosheon and thought it was okay because her face wasn't in the picture. What do you think?

7. Damika said that Rosheon was charged as a sexual predator, among other things, because she had sent an explicit picture of herself to his phone, and he shared it. Discuss.

8. What are some actions that Damika could have taken the first time Rosheon was rough with her?

9. Dana skipped her last period study hall because she saw it as not a real class? What do you think about this? Was she really skipping school?

10. Rosheon told Damika that oral sex was not sex. What do you think?

11. What are some ways that the situation with Michelle could have been handled?

12. What do you think of Dana's father's advice to take the high road? Would you have gone back to the church?

3/95399 - 7725

CPSIA information can be obtained at www.ICGtesting.com
Printed in the USA
LVOW08s0026160714

394545LV00001B/44/P